D1799445

2

KILLER

Douglas Heeney came out of prison harbouring a grudge against a certain Roy Denver because it was Denver who had been instrumental in having him arrested and sentenced for his part in a warehouse robbery. The fact that he deserved the punishment and that Detective Inspector Denver had simply been carrying out his duty in making the arrest made no difference as far as Heeney was concerned. During the years of his imprisonment the thought of how he would take his revenge on Denver had never been far from his mind. He had made plans, and the plans all pointed to one conclusion – the death of Roy Denver. And though Denver had left the police, Henney still intended to kill him, for he never forgot or forgave an injury, real or imagined.

But first there were a few other matters to attend to ...

KILLER

JAMES PATTINSON

ROBERT HALE · LONDON

© James Pattinson 1989
First published in Great Britain 1989

ISBN 0 7090 3453 9

Robert Hale Limited
Clerkenwell House
Clerkenwell Green
London EC1R 0HT

Photoset in North Wales by
Derek Doyle & Associates, Mold, Clwyd.
Printed in Great Britain by
WBC Print Ltd., Barton Manor, Bristol.
Bound by WBC Bookbinders Limited.

Contents

ONE

So Long, Dead Man

Roy Denver's car was held up in a traffic block in the approaches to Seaport's Haig Street Station when a man opened the door on the nearside and slipped into the passenger seat beside him.

'Hey!' Denver said. 'What do you think you're doing?' But then he took a closer look at the man and saw who it was who was sitting there and grinning at him.

'Remember me, Inspector?'

Denver remembered him; the face was unforgettable and he had seen enough of it a few years back to ensure that it would stay in his memory. More than enough, in fact.

'Duggie Heeney!'

'Right in one.' Heeney grinned again, but it was a vicious grin and did nothing to make the features more attractive. Not to Denver.

Yet he had to admit that there were people who might have a different opinion from his regarding Heeney's looks; women especially. That black hair, those slightly hollow cheeks, that long thin nose and the pointed chin, that dark shadow of stubble which could hardly be called a beard but was a kind of halfway stage between the shaven and the hirsute; all this might have its enchantment for the female of the species, or at least for some.

But Denver had looked into the hooded eyes and seen

7

the glint of something that turned his stomach; a hint of
madness perhaps; of criminal and even homicidal
madness. And whatever the headshrinkers might say, in
his estimation Heeney rated as a nut-case, and a
dangerous one at that.

'So they let you out?'

'Had to, didn't they? Done my time, less remission for
good behaviour and all that crap.'

'So you behaved yourself while you were inside?'

'Betcher sweet life, I did. I'm not stupid.'

'Stupid enough to get yourself put there in the first
place.'

The shaft went home; Denver could tell it had.
Heeney was still smiling, but the venom in him was only
thinly disguised by this outward show. He spoke
sarcastically.

'Let's put it another way. Let's say it was you as was a
bit too clever for me, Inspector.'

'Maybe it was at that,' Denver said. 'But you don't
have to call me inspector. I'm not with the Force any
more.'

Heeney showed no surprise. 'Ah, so I heard. What
happened? Did they kick you out? Find you was on the
take, doin' a bit of the old graft on the side or
something?'

Denver resisted the temptation to give Heeney a
bunch of knuckles in the teeth and got the blue Ford
Sierra moving with the traffic that had begun to flow
again.

'No, nothing like that. I left of my own free will.'

He was still not altogether certain it had been a wise
decision. Thirty-four years old and a detective
inspector, he might have looked forward to a successful
career in the Seaport police. Some people would have
said that he had thrown away an assured future for no
good reason; and maybe they would have been right.
But to his way of thinking there had been reasons

enough; for some time he had been unsettled; maybe he was too independent, too willing to bend the rules instead of going strictly by the book. It had got him into trouble with his superiors on more than one occasion and earned him a few raps over the knuckles. There had been friction with colleagues, too; back-biting and a lack of co-operation in certain quarters; so that, what with one thing and another, he had decided to call it a day while he was still young enough to make a fresh start.

He had talked it over with Valerie, and she had agreed that if that was the way he felt it was the best thing to do. She was certainly not going to urge him to stay on in a job he had come to dislike.

'Life's too short for that, Roy. We've got to make the most of it while we can.'

He was grateful for her support, though it was not unexpected; she was a very understanding person, as well as being lovelier than any other woman he knew.

He had made no immediate attempt to find another job; they were pretty hard to get anyway. Instead, he set up in business as a security consultant and became a free-lance agent for a firm which fitted window-locks, burglar-alarms and similar devices for outwitting the criminal fraternity. His income was uncertain and never amounted to what he had been earning as a detective inspector, but he was his own boss and nobody was looking over his shoulder and telling him what to do. He had no regrets. If the security caper failed to come up to expectations he would try some other line; there would surely be something he could turn his hand to, and he had no doubt that he would always be able to make a decent living in one way or another.

'So,' Heeney said, 'you're not a copper any more; just an ordinary private citizen like me and the next man.'

'No,' Denver said. 'Never like you. Never in a million years. You're dirt.'

He was giving all his attention to his driving and did

not observe the reaction of his passenger to this expression of contempt. Heeney's face darkened and he shot a look at Denver which did nothing to disguise the bitter hatred he felt for the ex-policeman. He had a struggle to control himself, because he felt an almost irresistible impulse to attack the man; and if he had had a knife he might have used it there and then and to hell with the consequences. So maybe it was as well that he was unarmed, because this was neither the time nor the place for anything of that kind. And there was no hurry; it could wait. Patience! That was all that was needed. The time would come.

So he took a grip on himself and kept his hands in his pockets, as though only in that way could he be certain that they would not act of their own volition and spoil everything by their impetuosity. And when he spoke it was softly, keeping the rancour out of his voice and merely giving it a faintly injured tone, as though he had been unjustly slandered.

'You didn't oughter say that, Mr Denver. It's an insult, you know, a diabolical liberty.'

'It's the truth,' Denver said. 'You're a shit. Scum like you pollute everything they touch. You're like a crawling slug leaving a slimy trail wherever you go.'

'Now, now, Mr Denver!' Heeney said; and try to suppress it as he might, a note of menace had crept into his voice, though he still spoke softly. 'You should mind what you're saying. You could get yourself into trouble, you know, real trouble.'

Denver shot a contemptuous glance at him. 'That wouldn't be a threat, would it?'

'A threat! Oh, no. I wouldn't presume to threaten a man like you. Not an insignificant person like me; you know that.' Heeney spoke with a thinly veiled sneer, overdoing the humility. 'It was just a word of advice.'

'You advising me! Now that really is something for the book.'

'No need to make such a big thing of it, Mr D. You think you don't need no advice?'

'Not from you.'

'Well, have it your own way. Whatcher bin doing since you left the coppers?'

'This and that.'

'And it's a living?'

'I get by. What are you aiming to do now you're out?'

'Now that's a question,' Heeney said. 'There's a load of jobs what've had to wait while my movements have been hampered, as you might say; jobs I couldn't get stuck into on account of little things like bolts and bars and high brick walls. You know what it's like to be shut up and not able to get out, Mr D?'

'Can't say I've ever had the experience,' Denver admitted. 'But I can imagine.'

'No, you can't. Nobody can. You have to take it first-hand to really know. It grinds you down; the monotony, the frustration, the sodding smell of it. You get to thinking about all sorts of things. Oh yes, you do a lot of thinking inside. But how would you know?'

'Well, there's no use whining. You had it coming to you. You should've kept your nose clean.'

'You going to read me a lecture on the evils of being a bad boy?'

'No,' Denver said. 'Because I know it would be a waste of time. You're set in your nasty little ways and nothing's going to alter you now.'

'And you aren't even going to try? I'm surprised at you, a good upright citizen like you.'

Denver ignored the sarcasm. 'Why should I? It's not my pigeon; not any more it isn't. I've finished with having to bother myself with villains like you.'

'I wouldn't be so bloody sure about that if I was you,' Heeney said softly.

Again Denver shot a swift questioning glance at him. They had left Haig Street now and were going up the slope of Exeter Street where the traffic was less congested. He had not asked Heeney where he wanted to go; the man had got into the car uninvited and he was free to get out of it again whenever he wished; but Denver had no intention of going out of his way to please his passenger.

'What's that supposed to mean?' he asked.

'Nothing.'

Denver did not believe him. Heeney was a mean bastard and he probably reckoned he had a score to settle, because he, Denver, was the man who had arrested him and had been instrumental in getting him sent to prison. So maybe he had something worked out in his warped little mind, something that entailed no kind of good for the ex-inspector.

'If you're thinking of getting your own back on me, you'd better forget it. You'll only be making more trouble for yourself.'

'And it don't worry you?'

Denver spoke scornfully. 'The day I start worrying about reprisals from garbage like you, Duggie, I'll be ready to hand in my chips.' He was not frightened by Heeney's vague hints of retribution; it was just talk; the man would do nothing.

And yet could he really be so certain of that? Might it not be prudent to take Heeney's words a little more seriously? In that piece of business for which he and three other men had been put away in Parkways Prison he had acted very savagely in resisting arrest and had inflicted severe injuries on two police officers. So it would be foolish to imagine that Heeney was at all averse to using violence when he felt inclined to do so; his past record refuted any such idea. Given suitable conditions, like a deserted alleyway on a dark night, he might indeed try something; a stealthy attack from behind would be just his kind of operation.

Well, then, this being so, it would be expedient to

ensure that the bastard was offered no such opportunity. He would be on his guard; and if Heeney was indeed planning anything it had been foolish to hand out a warning to his intended victim. But perhaps after all it was nothing but bluff, the purpose being to make Denver uneasy, even fearful. Perhaps he was laughing up his sleeve to think how his clever little ploy was going to put the other man's nerves on edge and give him sleepless nights wondering where and when the blow might fall.

'It won't work, you know, Duggie.'

'What won't, Mr D?'

'This little scheme of yours to get me running scared. We both know you haven't the guts to get yourself tangled with me.'

'Of course we do, Mr D. No need for a man like you to worry about dirt like me. You said it yourself; I'm a shit. Who'd be afraid of a shit?'

Denver detected mockery in Heeney's words, but he ignored it. 'Where have you been living since you came out?'

'With my old ma. Where else would I go?'

Denver could think of a lot of alternatives, but he did not say so. 'She's moved since you went inside, hasn't she?'

'That's right. She's got a luxury apartment now. A little bit of heaven on earth.'

Heeney was being sarcastic again. Denver knew that there was nothing heavenly about Mrs Heeney's present quarters except perhaps their height above the ground. She occupied a sixth floor council flat in one of those disastrous high-rise concrete blocks that had quickly deteriorated into the new perpendicular slums.

They were going up Calthorpe Hill now, past the old weathered buildings of the university. It was not on the way to Mrs Heeney's place.

'Where do you want me to drop you off?' Denver asked.

'Anywhere,' Heeney said. 'I only came along for the ride.'

'Well, don't make a habit of it, that's all.'

'You mean you don't enjoy my company?' Heeney asked in mock surprise, giving a lopsided grin. 'And there was me thinking you was loving our little heart-to-heart.'

'The only thing I really love about you,' Denver said, 'is your absence.' He pulled the car to a halt by the kerb. 'Here's where we say goodbye.'

Heeney opened the door and got out. He stood with one hand on the door looking in at Denver. 'Not goodbye, Mr D. Just aw-revaw. We'll meet again.'

'I hope not. You're a bastard, Duggie. For my money the judge was too lenient with you; he should have given you double the sentence. Personally, I'd have sent you down for life.'

'Good for you,' Heeney said. He slammed the door with a sudden flick of the hand, as though Denver's parting words had touched him on the raw and he was giving vent to some of the anger he had kept bottled up. 'Good for you, Mr Bloody Righteous.'

Denver cast one glance back at him as he took the car away. Heeney was standing on the kerb, not moving. He was wearing a dirty white T-shirt, a black leather jacket, faded blue jeans and a pair of well-worn training shoes. Denver thought he looked like a starving wolf. And maybe he was just as dangerous.

He could not hear what Heeney was saying as he watched the blue Sierra moving away up the hill; which was perhaps as well, since it might have disturbed him.

Heeney spoke through clenched teeth in a kind of low growl, so that his words would have been inaudible at a distance of more than a few feet, and there was no one close enough to hear him.

'So long to you, Mr D,' he said, 'until we meet again. So long, dead man!'

TWO
Punks

Oblivious of this parting shot from his recent passenger, Denver drove on and eventually came to the house where he lived and from which base he carried on his security business.

There was nothing very impressive about it; it was situated in one of the older residential districts which had been developed by speculative builders in the nineteen twenties and thirties. It was rather dilapidated and the garden had been allowed to run riot, but in the south of England it would probably have had an asking price of eighty thousand pounds or so. In this area where the recession had depressed property values such residences could be picked up for a great deal less.

He and Valerie had pooled their resources and bought it when they had decided some years ago that it would be a good idea to start living together. Complications might set in if they ever split up, but Denver hoped it would never come to that because he felt sure there was no other woman who could adequately have taken her place in his scheme of things. Nevertheless, she was quite a bit younger than he was, and in a few more years who could tell what the prospect might look like from her point of view? So perhaps ...

But having progressed so far along this particular

road of speculation he always pulled himself up pretty sharply, because there was no sense in carrying further an exercise which could lead to no positive conclusion and might simply result in a feeling of deep depression.

He parked the Sierra on the gravel that had become compacted with grass and weeds and let himself into the house by the front door, which was sheltered from the weather by a small porch. Valerie was in the kitchen preparing an evening meal, and she paused in this occupation to give him a welcoming kiss.

'You've got flour on your nose,' Denver said.

'It developed an itch and I had to scratch it. Don't let it bother you.'

There was flour on her hands also; she had kept them away from him during the kiss. She was wearing a striped cook's apron which was looped round her neck and tied in a large bow at the waist. He thought it gave her an attractively domestic appearance.

'It doesn't bother me,' he said. 'I rather like it. So the Whizzkid didn't keep you working late.'

'Not today. He had to get away early himself.'

The Whizzkid's real name was Kenneth Roper, and Miss Valerie West was his private secretary. Denver had given him, without his knowledge, the nickname, perhaps with some secret feeling of envy, because it could not be denied that Roper was a real go-getter. At the age of little more than thirty he was already a millionaire and still on the way up. The story was – and it could have been true – that he had started Micro Plastics with a capital of just one thousand pounds and in less than ten years had built it up into a successful industry with a multi-million pound turnover and a work force of some four hundred employees.

And there could be no doubt that Roper was good for Seaport: with the shipping trade a mere shadow of what it had once been and dozens of old factories closed down, bright new industries like Micro Plastics, which

could compete with and even beat the competition from
the Far East, were just what the City Fathers were
praying for. If only there had been a few more Ken
Ropers around the prospect for those who swelled the
dole queues and crowded the offices of the DHSS might
have been far rosier.

'He wants to have a talk with you,' Valerie said.

'With me! What about?'

'Security, of course. What else?'

'I don't know what else. Have you been twisting his
arm?'

Denver had a suspicion that Miss West had been
putting in some public relations work on his behalf, and
he was not at all sure that it pleased him. He was not
keen on having Roper throw some business in his
direction simply to gratify his private secretary. The
thought of being under any obligation to the Whizzkid
of all people was not a welcome one.

'I did suggest you might be worth consulting,' Valerie
said. 'I wouldn't call that twisting his arm.'

'Coming from you any suggestion might carry a lot of
weight, don't you think?'

'Well, goodness me!' she said. 'So what if it does!
Don't you want to pick up some extra business?'

'Of course I do, but I'd rather pick it up in my own
way, if you don't mind. I don't want Roper to dish out a
bit of employment for me just as a favour to you.'

'Oh, for God's sake, Roy! What crazy idea have you
got into your noddle?' Miss West spoke sharply and he
could tell she was annoyed by the way she was attacking
an inoffensive slab of dough on the pastry board. 'You
don't surely imagine he's going to hire your services
just because I work for him, do you? If he doesn't
believe you can give him good value for his money he'll
soon send you packing. He didn't get to be a
millionaire by throwing the stuff away.'

'I don't suppose he did.'

'Well, then –'

'All right,' Denver said. 'Let's not argue about it. It isn't worth a fight between you and me, is it? It's not that important.' He had no wish to quarrel with her, and in the end it would probably all come to nothing.

'And you'll go and talk to him if I arrange an appointment? You'll do that?'

'If it'll please you.'

She gave him a look that suggested she was not altogether satisfied with such a grudging acceptance, but she must have come to the conclusion that it would be best to drop the subject for the present and she said no more.

They were eating the meal at the kitchen table when he told her about the encounter with Duggie Heeney. She looked concerned.

'He threatened you?'

'In a guarded sort of way.'

'How do you mean?'

'He threw out a few hints that I might come to some harm. I got the impression that he holds me responsible for his spell in jail because I was the one who arrested him. I have no doubt he'd like to get his own back.'

'What do you think he'll do?'

'Nothing. When it comes to the point he won't have the nerve to do anything. He hates my guts of course, that's certain; and he's as mean as they come and vicious with it, but I'm not bothered about him.'

'Perhaps you should be.' She reached across the table and took his hand in hers, and he could tell that she was worried. In a way it pleased him, this concern for his welfare, because it indicated that he still meant a lot to her; and sometimes he had little teasing doubts about that.

When he looked at her and saw how lovely she was, with that silky brown hair and those lustrous eyes and all the other attributes of face and figure, he could not help wondering yet again whether the day might not come, sooner perhaps than later, when she would take stock of things and come to the conclusion that he was not the only pebble on the beach and that some of the others were a good deal more worth having. Every morning when he shaved his mirror reminded him that he was hardly a front runner in the handsome man stakes; he had never been even when younger, and now that his face had taken a bit of hammer from certain villains in the course of his detective duties it had a somewhat battered appearance.

So what could there be in him to retain her affection? What, indeed! There were surely plenty of other men around who had far more to offer than he had and would be happy to make a grab at her if given the slightest encouragement. He could think of one for a start without even trying: the Whizzkid. There could be no denying that Ken Roper had everything going for him: good looks, wealth, charm, comparative youth. And he was unattached apparently. Besides which, he had every opportunity to impress her with his eligibility, since he had her with him for five days in the week.

Denver tried not to let his mind dwell on the possibility that, even if it had not come to this at present, the relationship between Val and her employer might one day ripen into something a good deal closer than that of young tycoon and invaluable private secretary. It bothered him, and he had to admit it to himself if to no one else. In fact it bothered him a hell of a lot more than the possibility that Duggie Heeney might try to get his own back by some underhand means or other. With that threat to his person he could cope; with this other threat to the very mainspring of his existence he was not so sure that he could.

And yet he could not really be sure that there was any threat. Maybe it existed only in his own imagination. And then again, maybe not.

'There's no need for you to worry, Val,' he said.

'But I am worried. I'm afraid for you. You said yourself this man is vicious, and he feels he's got a grudge against you. So don't you think you ought to take some precautions?'

'Like what? Asking for police protection? That would really give them a laugh.'

'But it's no laughing matter, is it?'

'Look,' Denver said, 'it's like I told you; nothing will come of it. And there's no need to get into a lather. If I were to go running scared of every ex-con I've helped to put away I'd soon be a nervous wreck.'

He could see that he had failed to reassure her. She said: 'We're not talking about all the ex-cons; we're talking about one in particular.'

'Duggie Heeney is no different from the rest,' Denver told her. But he knew it was just not true. Heeney was a nutter, and nutters were unpredictable. Your ordinary criminal was interested only in the profit motive and accepted the risk of arrest and imprisonment as one of the hazards of the trade. He would have considered it a waste of time and energy to go looking for revenge on the man who had put the bracelets on him. But someone like Heeney might not even bother to count the cost in his desire for vengeance.

Valerie said no more about it. He had not convinced her; he knew that. But there was no point in arguing about it.

All the same, he was glad she cared.

The ex-con himself, having parted company with Roy Denver, uttered those ominous final words and turned away from the kerb. He then made his way to a public-house where he sat for most of the evening brooding over his beer, smoking cigarettes which he rolled for himself and eyeing the other customers with ill-concealed disdain. Generally speaking, he had no

great liking for his fellow human beings and seldom
went out of his way to make friends with anybody unless
it suited his purpose to do so.

A few of the people who came into the pub appeared
to recognise him and gave him the nod, but none of
them seemed eager to fraternise with him. Nobody
came over to ask him how he was getting on, and he had
no desire that they should do so. He could manage
without them, did not need them; they could go to the
devil for all he cared.

It was getting on for closing-time when he left the
public-house and began to make his way towards what,
for lack of a better term, he had to call home. There
were two ways you could get to the blocks of flats which
an eager council had erected when the future of
accommodation for the proletariat had appeared to be
with the pre-cast concrete section and the multi-storey
building. One way was by the road which was used by
wheeled vehicles, while the other was by a footpath
which cut across a piece of derelict ground where some
old factory buildings were still standing but were
gradually falling into decay.

This path was used more by day than by night; after
dark only the brave or the reckless walked that way,
because there was a distinct possibility of being set upon
by thugs or gangs of youths unless you were in a big
enough party to discourage such attacks. Drug addicts
and meths drinkers sometimes frequented the abandoned buildings, and there were stunted thorn bushes
and clumps of elder and bramble here and there.

Heeney left the metalled road and took this dark and
hazardous path without a moment's hesitation, though
he was well aware of the risk he ran. He just did not
care. No one was going to make him take the longer
route, no one.

But he took precautions; in the absence of a knife he
provided himself with another weapon. On his way into

town earlier in the day he had spotted a strip of rusty iron lying in the rough grass. It was flat and was about an inch wide and two feet long and there were some countersunk holes in the metal which seemed to have been made for screws, indicating that it might once have been used for strengthening purposes. He had picked it up and carried it with him to the point where the footpath came out on to the road, and there he had hidden it under a bush when no one was observing him.

Now as he stepped back on to the path he went to the bush which was no more than a shadowy object in the gloom and retrieved the weapon. With this grasped firmly in his hand he went on his way, alert and ready for any eventuality.

He covered more than half the distance to the tower block where his mother lived without encountering another person, and he had an odd feeling of disappointment, as though, having prepared himself for physical conflict, he had been let down. But then, as he was coming up to one of the derelict buildings, a big black shape on his right, three scarcely discernible figures appeared from this cover and took up a position on the path in front of him.

Heeney uttered a faint sighing exclamation: 'Ah!'

He came to a halt some five or six paces from them; and they were facing him, not moving. The light was poor, but he could see that they had cropped heads and were wearing skin-tight faded jeans tucked into lace-up boots. It was as if they had been waiting for him, as if they had known he would be coming. It was as if they were looking for trouble; and maybe they had found it; found more than they had ever bargained for.

Heeney laughed softly, inwardly, exultingly, the sound almost inaudible in the still night. He was holding the iron rod behind his back so that it was invisible to the other three.

One of the skinheads broke the silence: 'Where you

think you're goin'?'

'I don't think,' Heeney said, speaking in a low controlled voice. 'I know. I'm going home.'

'So you got a home! Well, think of that now. Who'd have believed it?'

The other two sniggered, so maybe this passed for wit in their book.

'Are you going to let me pass?' Heeney asked; still calm, still keeping it polite; ominously so.

'You gotta pay first,' the skinhead said. He seemed to be the leader, the one who did the talking. 'This is a toll-path. Didn't you know?'

'And you collect the toll?'

'That's right.'

'How much is it?'

'All you got on you.'

'So I give you all I've got and you let me pass? Is that it?'

'Not quite. Then we think about it. If you don't have enough on you maybe we take it out of you some other way.'

'Is that a fact? Like carving me up a little here and there, maybe?'

'You're smart,' the skinhead said. 'You got it right in one.'

Heeney saw that he was carrying a knife in his hand. The one on his left also had a knife, while the one on the other side appeared to be wearing something on his right hand which looked remarkably like a knuckleduster with spikes.

Nice boys!

'You punks!' Heeney said, no longer in the mock polite tones he had used until now but spitting out the words with disdain. 'You miserable stinking punks!' He was not afraid; he had handled tougher babies than these in stir. Some of them had imagined he was easy, a pushover; they had discovered it was not so; he knew how to take care of himself. After that they had left him alone. He was no mixer and he was nobody's man but his own.

The skinheads were momentarily taken aback by this sudden change in the attitude of their intended victim. They hesitated, as if uncertain how to react. Heeney gave them no time to make up their minds; he brought the length of iron from behind his back and went on to the attack.

They were not expecting it and did not immediately respond. Heeney went for the one in the middle, the one who had done the talking. He made a sweep with the iron and the edge of it caught the skinhead on the wrist just above the hand that was holding the knife. There was a sharp cracking sound which might have been a bone breaking. The skinhead gave a howl and dropped the knife.

The other one with a knife made a lunge at Heeney, but Heeney was too quick for him and gave him a poke in the throat with the end of the iron rod. It stopped him in his tracks, but there was still the one with the knuckleduster. Heeney turned and caught a glimpse of the metal spikes coming at his face. He ducked away but was just too late to avoid the blow completely; he felt one of the points scratch his chin.

It was like the nick made by a razor when shaving, nothing, a little blood: but it angered him, made him really venomous. He brought his knee up into the skinhead's crotch, which caused the man to double up in pain. While he was in that position Heeney delivered a blow with the iron rod to the back of the neck which knocked him to the ground, where he lay dazed and groaning. Heeney kicked him in the ribs to give him something more to groan about and stepped back to survey the situation.

The other two were making no move to come at him again. The one who had done the talking was holding his right arm with his left hand and he seemed to be in pain. The one Heeney had prodded in the throat was also feeling his injury, to judge by the sounds he was making.

Heeney spoke mockingly: 'Well, come on then. Don't tell me you've had enough. Not already. Why, we've hardly begun as yet.' He swung the rod in an arc like a man wielding a sabre, cutting the air, as if to demonstrate what he could do should the need arise. 'Besides, there's that toll you was talking about; not been collected yet, has it? Which one of you's going to step forward and pick my pockets?'

None of them moved. The one on the ground had made an attempt to get up but he was still on his hands and knees, head drooping. The one with the damaged wrist had not yet picked up his knife. In less than a minute Heeney had tamed all three of them and they no longer had any eagerness for a fight. They just watched him sullenly as he savaged the air with the weapon in his hand.

'Well,' he said, 'if you've got no more to say to me I'll be on my way. I can't stick around here all night. You better get off the path or I might walk right over you. Okay?'

They moved aside to let him pass; even the one on the ground crawled away. Heeney walked jauntily past them. He was still on the alert, guessing that they might come up from behind and attack him in the rear; but they made no move to do so.

Ten paces on he turned and spoke to them. 'You wanter know who I am? I'm Duggie Heeney. Remember that. Heeney. Nobody interferes with me, nobody.'

Maybe the word would get around. Older people might remember the name; he hadn't been away that long, damn it! But these punks; they'd been no more than kids when he'd gone away. Well, they knew about him now; he had given them a lesson they were not likely to forget in a hurry.

He walked on again. He heard the one with the bad wrist shout: 'Heeney!' He stopped and faced them. The distance made them merge into the darkness, shadows that were barely visible.

'We'll get you, Heeney.' The voice was hoarse, savage, almost hysterical. 'We'll make you pay for this, see if we don't.'

Heeney thought of going back. Maybe he had not taught them the lesson well enough; maybe he ought to give them some more punishment.

But they were not worth it. They might talk big, hand out threats, but deep down there was nothing to them, nothing.

'Punks!'

He turned again and went on his way, swinging the iron rod like a walking-stick.

'Punks!'

THREE
Decision

He came out on to the road still carrying the iron. There were street-lamps here and there, but very few people about and little traffic. The blocks of flats stood up like monstrous growths, some windows showing lights, others dark.

Heeney crossed a piece of waste ground and came to the entrance to the block where his mother lived. A gang of kids had congregated there and they were making enough noise to waken the dead; shouting, kicking things around and swearing like little troopers. Heeney came to a halt and looked at them. He knew who they were; his mother had told him about them; they terrorised the older people in the flats, vandalised everything they could lay their hands on and made a general nuisance of themselves.

They seemed to be under no parental control, played truant from school and got up to all kinds of mischief. The police did little about the problem; maybe they had too many other engagements and considered a lot of kids not worth bothering about. Mrs Heeney never went out of the flat after dark; she was afraid to, what with these young gangsters and the muggers. And there were others like her; they just locked their doors and hoped no one would break in.

None of the kids noticed Heeney at first. Then one of

27

them saw him and drew the attention of the others.

'Look who's here!'

They all went suddenly quiet and stared at him.

Heeney said nothing.

One of the boys said: 'What you want, mister?' He was bigger than most of the others and he could have been the gang leader. He had tow-coloured hair and a snub nose and a crop of pimples like pebbles on a beach. He spoke with a touch of arrogance, as though daring Heeney to make a move.

'I want you lot out of here,' Heeney said. 'Beat it.'

'Sod you!' the boy said. 'Who's talking?'

'I am,' Heeney said.

'And who might you be when you're at home?'

'Never mind who I am. Are you going or aren't you?'

The kids behind the tow-haired boy were silent. Heeney could sense the expectancy in them. They were watching their leader, waiting to see how he handled the situation, their own actions dependent on his.

'You think you can make us go, mister?' the boy asked; sneering, taunting Heeney.

'Look,' Heeney said, not raising his voice, just sounding the faintest bit tired, 'I just dealt with three punks who thought they could mug me. They were tougher than all you lot put together; they had knives and knuckledusters. One of 'em will need hospital treatment, maybe two of 'em.' He tapped the concrete underfoot with the iron rod and it made a dull metallic sound. 'Do you want me to deal with you kids too?'

The boy stood his ground for perhaps five seconds, looking into Heeney's eyes; then he lost his nerve.

'Come on. Why waste our time here?'

He walked past Heeney with a kind of self-conscious swagger, trying to make out he was not afraid, that he would have had it out with Heeney if he had felt so inclined but that it was just not worth the bother.

The others followed him meekly, not making a sound.

Heeney gave that inward exultant laugh of his which seemed to be lost somewhere in the region of his chest and walked to the lift.

The lift was in working order, which was not always so. It broke down fairly frequently and had periods of inaction when the dwellers on the upper floors had to make their way up and down long flights of concrete stairs. Some of them were not physically capable of this kind of exercise and had to rely on other people to do their shopping. They had never had problems like this in the old terrace houses from which they had been moved in the name of social progress.

Vandals armed with aerosol cans had left obscene graffiti on the interior of the lift. It was perhaps a measure of that same social progress that what had once been executed with pencil and chalk was now more permanently carried out with an instant spray of liquid paint. Only the puerile minds of the compulsive defilers of public property had made no advance in the course of the centuries: the wit was still basic.

On Heeney these daubs made no impression; he was oblivious of them. As long as the lift worked he was bothered neither by the mural decorations nor the dirt underfoot nor even the lingering odour of human urine that pervaded this small cubicle in which he was being hoisted to the sixth floor of the building.

He had his own key to his mother's flat and he let himself in. She was in the living-room with the television on, but she was not looking at it. Heeney walked across the room and switched it off. He still had the length of iron in his hand and his mother caught sight of it at once.

'What you got there, Dug?'

'This? Oh, just something I picked up.' He stood the rod in a corner.

'What you mean, you picked it up? What you want a bit of old rusty iron for?' Mrs Heeney sounded querulous. She was a fat untidy woman in her middle sixties, her grey hair cut in a fringe and a pair of metal-rimmed glasses perched on her blob of a nose. She was wearing a grubby pinafore and carpet slippers and her ankles were dropsical. She was sitting in an old armchair with worn and greasy upholstery and there was an ashtray full of cigarette butts on a small table near her elbow.

'Protection,' Heeney said.

She noticed the blood on his chin. 'You been in a fight, son?'

'I'd hardly call it that. Some punks started something they couldn't finish. I had to learn them a lesson, not to take liberties with me. Then there was a gang of kids downstairs. I sent them packing.'

'Little bastards! Allus causing trouble. Don't know what things is coming to these days. What with the glue-sniffing and the drug-taking and that, you don't know where you are. Weren't like that at the old place; there you had proper neighbours what you could trust; you knew everybody in the street and there was a pub on the corner where you could go nights. Now you don't dare move outside; you have to sit by yourself in this bloody place what's cold and damp and draughty and miles above the ground. It ain't right. What are the coppers doing about it?'

'What've the coppers got to do with your draughts and damp?' Heeney asked.

'I don't mean that; you know I don't. I mean them little hooligans and the muggers and all. Why don't they do something? It's what they're paid for, isn't it?'

'I don't know what they're paid for.' Heeney sounded impatient. 'You better forget about the bastards; they never done me no good. Nor you neether, for that matter. And they're all on the take.'

'Well, all I know is things used to be better in the old days.' Mrs Heeney was embarked on her long list of grievances which her son had heard before. She reached for a cigarette and lit it. 'When I was young you wasn't afraid to go out for a nice evening's entertainment and the kids behaved theirselves. It was nice then.' She began to cough wheezingly. 'I liked them little houses. Why'd they have to go and pull 'em down and shove us in these here concrete towers? If we'd been meant to live in the sky we'd have been given wings and we'd have built our nests in trees.'

'Some nest you'd've built,' Heeney said. 'You'd've had to give up the fags too, else you'd've set light to it.'

His own memory of the old terrace house where he had been born and brought up was not as rosy as his mother's. He had never had any love for it and would have had no desire to return to it even if it had still been in existence. As he remembered it, it had been a proper little pigsty, because Mrs Heeney had never been one to keep a place clean and tidy wherever she might have been. It was small and cramped and the fire smoked and the privy was in a yard at the back in a sort of brick hovel. If you went out there after dark you had to take a lantern or a torch and there might be rats to give you a welcome. Periodically the men came with the night-soil cart emptying the buckets, and then you needed to keep your windows shut because the stench was unbelievable. There was no bathroom, just a cold-water tap over the earthenware sink and a tin bath hanging on the privy wall, which you took into the kitchen and filled with kettles.

And that was what the old woman was pining for!

Heeney could scarcely remember his father. Daniel Heeney was a seaman and was away from home for months on end, voyaging to romantic-sounding places in distant parts of the world. When he came back he would bring souvenirs like ebony elephants and copper trays and little carved ivory idols and pictures made with butterfly wings, which Mrs. Heeney might still have had if she had not pawned them long ago and never reclaimed them.

Heeney was about three years old when his father set off on another voyage and never came back. That was the last they ever saw or heard of him. When he grew older Heeney could understand why his father should have decided to take off like that: Norah Heeney had not been bad-looking when young, but she was a slut and maybe Daniel had grown tired of returning to that slummy nest. Maybe he had jumped ship in some far-off port and started a new life where the air was cleaner and the prospects brighter. Maybe he had hitched up with some seductive female in the mysterious Orient. Who could tell?

After the departure of his real father there were other men in Heeney's life; honorary uncles who lived in the house for varying periods of time. Some of them treated him well enough, some tried to ignore him, a few tormented him. He hated them all.

The last of these uncles was a man named Walter Brown, and he was the worst of the lot, an utter swine. For a start he was decently enough behaved, but gradually things deteriorated and he began to abuse Norah Heeney, physically as well as verbally. He was most violent when the pair of them had been down to the Blackamoor's Head for the evening and he had had too much to drink. He never hit her when they were out, but when they came back to the house he would start on her, so that sometimes she would be nursing a black eye or a cut lip for days.

Walter Brown was a stevedore, a big bull of a man, running to fat. Douglas Heeney was thirteen years old when this latest in the series moved into the house, and perhaps because he was approaching adolescence he hated this one more than any of the others. It was true that there had never been any very loving relationship between him and his mother; he guessed that to her he was more of a nuisance than anything else; she tolerated him because she had to and he tolerated her because he was not yet old enough to provide for himself; but there was no love. Nevertheless, he felt resentful that this great slob should just walk in and take a place at the kitchen table and in the bed upstairs as if he owned the property and all that went with it.

And then there was the way Brown treated him; always on at him for one thing or another; sneering at him, calling him dirty names, giving him cuffs on the ears for no reason at all. And a cuff on the ear from Walter Brown was no laughing matter; it was enough to knock your head sideways and give you a crick in the neck as well. It would bring the tears to his eyes, and then Brown would call him a cry-baby, a sissy, a spineless brat.

'When are you going to grow up to be a man, kid? When are you going to get some spirit into you? You can't be a mammy's boy all your life, you know.'

This last taunt was always enough to rouse Heeney to a fury, because it was so unjust. That was one thing he had never been, a mammy's boy; even if he had been inclined that way he would have been given no encouragement; he had been brought up to fend for himself and he guessed it was always going to be like that.

Mrs Heeney never made any attempt to defend her son in these confrontations. Heeney believed she was afraid of Walter Brown; and maybe after the first few weeks she regretted ever having let him make his home with her. But she lacked the courage to send him packing and endured the ill-treatment apparently with never a thought that she could have put a stop to it at once if only she had made a stand. She was after all the legal tenant; she paid the rent and Brown was there only on sufferance.

But he continued to live there and matters became progressively worse. One night when Brown and Mrs Heeney came back from an evening at the Blackamoor's Head they had not been two minutes inside the house before the trouble started. It was triggered off by the fact that Douglas Heeney was still up and about. Any excuse would have served, but Brown, in his state of drunken belligerence, decided to pick on this one.

'You little bastard! Why ain't you in bed?'

Heeney answered sullenly: 'What's it to you? You're not my dad.'

'Why you cheeky little devil!' Brown took a swipe at Heeney, but the boy was too quick for him and dodged out of the way. Brown was none too steady on his feet and fell heavily against the table, sending it crashing over with everything that was on it.

'Now see what you done,' Mrs Heeney scolded. 'Do you want to break everything in the house?'

Brown immediately turned on her. 'You keep your nose outa this. It's a matter atween me and that cocky young swine there.'

'Well, you oughter be more careful with the furniture.' Mrs Heeney righted the table and started picking things up from the floor, grumbling querulously and more than a little tipsy herself.

Brown focused his attention once again on Heeney. 'Come here, kid.'

'You go to hell,' Heeney said; scared but defiant.

Brown made a bull-like charge at him, head down. Heeney easily avoided him and he crashed into the wall, bringing down some plaster. The dust got into his throat and he began to cough, which immobilised him for the moment.

Mrs Heeney moved across and examined the patch of wall from which the plaster had fallen out and started complaining again. 'Now look! We'll have to get the builders in. What's that going to cost?' She gave Brown a push with her hand, oblivious of the danger of provoking him further.

He reacted instantly with a sweep of the arm which caught her in the stomach and doubled her up.

'Outa my way, you bitch!'

A stream of yellowy liquid gushed from her mouth and splashed on the floor. Brown grabbed her by the hair and hit her on the side of the face. He released her and she sank to the floor, moaning. He took a kick at her and almost overbalanced, missing his target. He staggered and his shoulder struck the wall, bringing down more of the plaster. He gave a shake of the head as if to clear it and looked for the boy.

Heeney could have got out of the room; he could have retreated upstairs; but he knew he would find no refuge there because Brown would follow him and there was no lock on the bedroom door. He might have run out into the street, but where would he have gone? And besides, there was a kind of fascination which held him there. Somehow he had to watch, had to see what Brown would do to the woman.

Brown spotted him and made another rush, and this time he caught Heeney in a corner. He thrust out a solid left arm and pinned the boy against the wall. Heeney, with the courage of desperation, kicked his assailant on the shin, but this merely served to enrage the big stevedore; he was used to shifting heavy cargoes around in the holds of ships and fleshy as he might be he had the muscle necessary for the job. Heeney was a scrawny kid, a mere flyweight in comparison with the man.

Brown started hitting him and he had no defence; when he put his hands up to fend off the blows they were swept aside. Brown went on hitting, hitting.

Mrs Heeney had got herself off the floor and was clawing at the stevedore's jacket, trying futilely to pull him away from the boy, screaming at him to stop.

'Leave him, Walter, leave him for God's sake! You'll

kill him.'

The words must finally have got through to Brown's drink-sodden brain; or maybe he had just grown weary of the exercise. Heeney had slipped down the wall and was crumpled up in the corner. Brown stepped back from him, breathing heavily.

'That'll learn you! Cocky young bastard!'

Heeney was barely conscious; his body felt as though it were nothing more than a receptacle for pain. But there was hatred in him too, burning, all-consuming; hatred of the man who had done this to him.

It was then that he came to a decision which was to prove a turning-point in his life; then that he knew for a certainty that one day, no matter what else might happen, he would have to kill Walter Brown.

FOUR
All In Good Time

Nevertheless, although the decision had been made on that fateful night, nearly another year was to pass before Heeney took any action to put his project into effect.

Not that he ever forgot it or even considered the possibility of abandoning it; for even if he had been at all inclined to do so, the continual persecution that he and his mother suffered under the dictatorship of the entrenched stevedore would have served to keep him dedicated to the ultimate realisation of the object he had in mind. Indeed, his resolve became ever firmer as the days went by, and he delayed only because he needed to be convinced that he could do what he intended doing with no risk of failure. Brown must die; of that there could be no question; but he had to die in such a way that there could be no chance of the killer being detected and brought to book. Therefore, there had to be no ill-judged haste; everything had to be carefully thought out; and only when the correct time arrived must the job be done.

It was probable that if she could have done so without trouble, Mrs Heeney would have got rid of Brown. In theory all she had to do was to tell him to pack his bags and go; but in practice this was impossible since she lacked the strength of will. All the men she had brought into the house in the past had been able to manipulate her with ease, and they had departed of their own free-will because they had tired of the liaison, not because she had told them to go.

Walter Brown was different from his predecessors, not only in the brutality he brought to the relationship but also in the fact that he stayed longer and apparently had no desire to leave. Sometimes Mrs Heeney talked of throwing him out, of going to the police and complaining about his behaviour; but he simply laughed in her face, knowing only too well that she would do nothing.

'You don't want to get rid of me, you know you don't. You need a man about the house.'

'I don't need you,' she said, but without conviction.

'Sure you do. You wouldn't know what to do with yourself without me.'

'I'd manage.'

Heeney knew as well as Brown that his mother would do nothing about turning the stevedore out of the house; she would just let things slide, as she always had. So it was up to him to take the necessary action. And he would when the time was ripe; that was certain. And for every cuff that Brown gave him and every sneering jibe that he threw at him Heeney's resolve became that much stronger. Let the bastard wait; oh, just let him wait! It was all coming to him. All in good time.

And it did come. In early December.

Brown had fallen into the habit of going to the Blackamoor's Head by himself, no longer taking Mrs Heeney with him. At first she had made some half-hearted objections to being left at home while he went out to enjoy himself, but he had told her to shut her mouth or he would shut it for her, and she had accepted the situation with her usual weak-willed resignation.

Heeney observed this new arrangement with satisfaction; it fitted in very nicely with a plan that had been taking shape in his mind. He began to make a close study of Brown's movements and discovered that he was a creature of habit: he would almost invariably stay at the public-house until closing-time and then would make his somewhat unsteady way back to the house.

At first there might be some drinking pals with him, but they would soon go their separate ways after leaving the pub, and for the last part of his journey Brown would be on his own. Taking a short cut he would walk through a narrow alleyway between two high walls which was completely dark on moonless nights except for what little light crept in from the roads at each end. It was here that Heeney proposed to waylay the stevedore.

Heeney was now fourteen years old, thin but wiry, and he was already embarked on a criminal career. He had become a petty thief and he knew a man who would buy anything he had to sell. This man, a Mr Alfred Waite, had a shop in a dingy side-street where he carried on his trade as a jeweller and pawnbroker; but Heeney had never entered the premises by the front door; there was a way in through a backyard which clients of his type used when they had goods to sell. You rang a bell three times and you were let into a musty little room cluttered with all kinds of junk where Mr Waite, a crook-backed hawk-faced man in a greasy black suit, carried on his clandestine business as a small-time fence.

Heeney had quickly become adept at this way of making a bit of pocket-money to spend on cigarettes and the slot-machines in the amusement arcades. His mother gave him a little money when she had any to spare; but that was not often, and it would have been worse than useless to dun Walter Brown for a hand-out; that would have simply been asking for a slap in the face.

But now Heeney knew that he was about to take a major step up the ladder of criminality, for there was a world of difference between petty larceny and murder; with murder you jumped right into the big league, and after that things could never be the same again.

Yet he did not hesitate; he went about his preparations coldly and methodically, untroubled by any qualms of conscience or any fears that his plan might end in disaster. It was simple and straightforward, without unnecessary frills, and if he carried it out with resolution he felt certain that nothing could go wrong.

He had given a deal of thought to the choice of a weapon, for this was important. He had considered the possibility of using an ordinary hammer, but had rejected the idea. If you used a hammer you had to take it away and clean the blood off it, or you had to get rid of it in some way; and there was always the possibility of some clever police detectives tracing the implement back to its source. He could have taken a hammer from the house; there was one that was used for breaking up lumps of coal; or he could have bought one at an ironmonger's shop; but either way he put himself at risk. The same objections applied to several other possible weapons, and in the end he settled on a common building brick such as you could pick up almost anywhere and could leave at the scene of the crime without fear that it might lead the investigators to the person who had used it.

He was well aware of the necessity of leaving no fingerprints which could provide damning evidence, and he bought a pair of cheap cotton gloves of the kind people used for working in the garden or around the house. Beyond this there was little else that needed to be done.

On the day which he had chosen for the operation he left the house at a quarter to ten in the evening. He had scrubbed the brick thoroughly to remove any trace of his fingerprints and had wrapped it in brown paper so that it looked like a small parcel. He carried it down from his bedroom concealed under his jacket so that his mother should not see it and want to know what it was. She was sitting by the fire, smoking a cigarette and reading a grubby women's magazine that was six months out of date, but she looked up when he came into the room.

'You going out, Duggie?'

'Yes.'

'Where you going?'

'Ask no questions and you'll be told no lies,' Heeney said.

'You're always going out late these days.' She spoke scoldingly. 'A boy of your age; 'tisn't safe.'

Heeney turned on her a faintly mocking glance. 'You think I might come to some harm?'

'I don't know. Anything could happen. You'd be better staying at home.'

'You're not going to forbid me to go out, are you?'

He was still making fun of her and she knew it. She knew he would go his own sweet way regardless of anything she might say. She had no control over him nowadays.

'Oh, go along with you. Will you be gone very long?'

'I don't expect so,' Heeney said; and he left her to her cigarettes and her magazine.

Having stepped out of the house he made his way without undue haste to the alleyway and walked down the length of it to the far end. Here he turned to the right, crossed the road and took up his position beside a tree which, against all the odds, was managing to stay alive at the edge of the pavement. From this position he was able to see the entrance to the alleyway to which he expected Walter Brown to come before so very long on his way back from the Blackamoor's Head.

It was a frosty moonless night and a layer of fog had settled on the town, blanketing everything with its chilling dampness. Heeney was wearing only a denim

jacket over a sweater and shirt, but he scarcely noticed
the cold, in spite of the lack of a coat; he had something
more important to think about, something that was
large enough to blot out any other consideration.

He had taken the wrapping off the brick and stuffed
it into one of his pockets and had laid the brick at the
foot of the tree. He was wearing the cotton gloves and
had not handled the brick with his bare fingers since
cleaning it.

One person went by on the other side of the road,
collar turned up, shoulders hunched, hurrying; Heeney
could hear the rapid clicking of the shoes and guessed
that the figure was a woman's. Most of the windows in
the houses were dark and this little-used side-street
appeared to be dead at that hour; it was the kind of
night for staying indoors by the fire.

He heard Walter Brown's heavy tread before the man
was anything more than a vague shadow in the fog and
could not be unmistakably identified. Then he came
into the light of a street-lamp and Heeney was sure; that
big hulking shape was the man he was waiting for and
could be none other.

Heeney drew back behind the tree, though he
doubted whether Brown would have noticed him even
if he had not done so. The stevedore was weaving
slightly from side to side, but he was moving at a good
pace and a few moments later he had vanished down
the alleyway.

Heeney picked up the brick and began to run, lightly
and soundlessly in his rubber-soled shoes. He came to
the alleyway and went in not far behind Brown. There
were cobblestones underfoot and the fog was freezing
on them, making them slippery with ice. Suddenly
Brown's feet shot from under him and he went down
with a heavy thud, cursing.

This was a bonus for Heeney. He had planned to
overtake Brown and trip him from behind, but this was

no longer necessary, since he was already down. He was starting to get himself up when Heeney reached him and struck him on the back of the head with the brick. The blow knocked him flat on his face and Heeney hit him again and again, hearing the bone of the skull crunch under the force of the impact.

He dropped the brick and slipped a hand into the pocket where he knew Brown kept his wallet. There was still a wad of paper money in the folder, and Heeney took the money and let the wallet fall to the ground beside the body so that it would look as if the motive for the killing had been simple robbery, a mugging that had perhaps gone too far.

He wasted no more time but began to run, leaving the dead man lying in the alleyway. He reached home without seeing another person.

There was blood on the cotton gloves, and before going in he took them off and wrapped them in the paper he had removed from the brick. When he walked in his mother was still sitting by the fire as he had left her; it was as though time had stood still.

She glanced up from the magazine. 'Oh, it's you. I thought it was Walter.'

'No,' Heeney said, 'it's not him.' He reached past her and dropped the paper-wrapped gloves into the fire, and he noticed that some of the blood had soaked through on to the fingers of his right hand.

'What was that?' Mrs Heeney asked.

'Just something I got no more use for,' Heeney said. 'Nothing for you to bother your head about.'

The paper had flared up and was blazing. As it burned the gloves became visible, but they were burning quickly too. Heeney picked up the poker with his left hand and stirred the ashes of the paper and the cotton so that they mingled with the glowing coals, making sure that all trace of them was destroyed.

Mrs Heeney noticed the blood on his right hand. 'You

cut yourself, Duggie?'

Heeney glanced at his fingers. 'Looks like it, don't it?'

'How'd you do that?'

'Never mind,' he said. 'Forget it.'

He went into the kitchen and washed his hands under the cold-water tap, making a thorough job of it with a cake of yellow soap. He examined his clothes to make sure that no blood had splashed on them and could find none. He dried his hands on the roller-towel and went back into the living-room.

'Where you been?' Mrs Heeney asked.

'Nowhere,' he said. 'I been here all evening. You should know that.'

He felt no remorse for what he had done, but rather a sense of immense elation. That he, a boy of fourteen, should have killed a man, and such a man as Walter Brown, was a marvellous thing; it gave him a feeling of power. Twenty minutes ago Brown was alive, a drunken sadistic brute; now he was dead. And it was he, Douglas Heeney, who had made him so, had snuffed out his life as a god might have done, with the stroke of his hand. Was not that really something to shout about?

But he kept himself under control, revealed no emotion, spoke calmly. 'I never went out of the house.'

'What you mean, never went out?'

'I mean if anyone asks, that's what you tell 'em. I been sitting in here all the time with you. Understand?'

She began to get an inkling of his meaning and she looked scared. 'You went an' done something out there, didn't you?'

'I didn't do anything out there. How could I if I never went out?'

'Suppose somebody saw you?'

'Nobody did see me.' He had made certain of that, both leaving and returning. 'Now have you got it? I was here with you, see?'

'Well, if you say so.' She sounded doubtful, confused

and far from happy.

'I do say so.' He was putting pressure on her. His was the stronger character and he knew that he could bend her to his will; that in future it would always be so even though he was yet only a boy. In future there would be no Walter Brown standing in his way; all that was finished.

It seemed that Mrs Heeney was also thinking of the stevedore. She said: 'I wonder where Walter is. He's usually back by this time.'

'Don't you bother yourself about him,' Heeney said. 'As likely as not he's had a skinful and is sleeping it off somewhere. Dead drunk.'

He could have left out the final word, told her that Brown was dead, full stop! That he was lying in an alleyway with his skull crushed by a brick. But she would learn all about that soon enough.

She worried at it. "Tisn't like him. He's always come home whatever state he's been in.'

'Do you want him home?' Heeney inquired, with a faint sneer. 'Do you love him that much? He treats you so well, don't he?'

She made no answer to that. She was smoking another cigarette and the ash had fallen on her dress. He reflected that there was a grubby slatternly look about her. She was pushing forty now and letting herself go. He felt no affection for her; he despised her; but she still had her uses.

'Why don't you go to bed,' he said. 'No sense in waiting up for him. He won't thank you for it.'

'He'll be expecting me to. He'll want a bite of something to eat.'

Heeney laughed harshly. 'Don't kid yourself. Look, I'll make a bet he don't never come in tonight. There!'

The confident manner in which he spoke made an impression on her. She looked at him questioningly. 'How can you be so sure? Do you know where he is?'

She glanced at the fire where the faint traces of the bundle he had thrown on to the coals were still just detectable. Then she looked at his right hand, clean now and with no sign of a cut where the blood had been. And gradually a thought seemed to creep into her mind, a terrible frightening thought, scarcely to be entertained because it was so unbelievable. The scared expression was on her face again, more marked now. Her lips trembled.

'Oh, my God!' She put a hand to her mouth. 'Oh, my God, Duggie! You never –'

He answered impatiently: 'No, I never. Don't go getting ideas into your head, cause it won't do, you know. I was here, remember. All evening.'

'Oh, Duggie, Duggie!' She had dropped the cigarette in the hearth and was shaking. 'Duggie, what are we going to do?'

He seized her by the shoulders and thrust his face close to hers. 'We're not going to do nothing; we don't have to. Just bear in mind I was here all the evening, that's all. Never forget that.'

He wondered whether he could trust her not to break down under questioning, trust her to say nothing about the burning of the gloves and about the blood on his hand. She was so damned weak; she might spill it all.

'You could be in trouble too,' he said. 'You know that, don't you?'

'Oh, Duggie!' she said again, and he could see that she was crying, the tears coursing down her cheeks. The stupid bitch! It made him angry with her, angry that he had to rely on such a poor brainless creature for an alibi. Suppose she let him down! Suppose she dropped him right in muck! What then? Christ!

Well, there was no point in worrying himself about that; he would just have to wait and see how things turned out, hoping for the best because the worst was just too bad to contemplate.

'It'll be all right,' he said. 'Everything is going to be okay. Things are going to be a lot better from now on. You'll see.'

And he just hoped he had not got it wrong.

FIVE
Pick-Up

He and his mother went to the funeral. She said it might look bad if they stayed away, and she could have been right at that. She even bought a black outfit for the occasion and shed some tears over the grave. But she had always been one for a good weep and any excuse would do.

Heeney wore no black clothes, or even a black armband, and he remained dry-eyed. There was no sense in making too much of a pantomime of it.

In the event he need not have worried about the questions that Mrs Heeney had to answer. The police came, but it was no more than a matter of routine because it was known that Walter Brown had been living with her. No policeman in his right mind would have suspected her of smashing a man's skull in with a brick, and it was obvious that they had no suspicions regarding Douglas Heeney either. He believed they would not have asked where he had been even if his mother, with an excess of eagerness to carry out his instructions to the letter, had not volunteered the information that he had been with her all the evening; and he was none too pleased to have their attention drawn to him in this way. It was as though she were making a point of the fact that he might need an alibi and putting the idea into their heads.

But they were really not interested; in their book the crime was a plain and simple mugging and they were not looking for a fourteen-year-old boy as the prime suspect.

When they had gone Heeney turned on his mother. 'You stupid old cow! Why'd you have to tell them that about me?'

'But you said I was to, Duggie. You said I wasn't to forget. And I didn't.' She sounded hurt, like a child that had imagined it had behaved well and had received not praise but a scolding.

'I didn't say you were to tell them if they didn't ask. You made it seem like you thought they oughter suspect me. Telling 'em like that might've made them start thinking I had something to hide.'

'I'm sorry, Duggie. I didn't think –'

'No, you never do, do you? Anyway, I reckon it's turned out all right. There won't be no trouble.'

There were some people at the funeral he had never seen before; Brown's relations, he supposed. They glanced with a hint of disapproval at Mrs Heeney, but they made no approach and did not speak to her.

Nobody came back with them to the house afterwards; there were no ham sandwiches and port wine for the mourners. Brown and Mrs Heeney had not after all been husband and wife, and any get-together after the ceremony would have been unthinkable. What would she have had to talk about with all those strangers?

From that time forward Heeney took over as the man of the house; it was as though at the age of fourteen he had suddenly acquired adulthood. He had gained an ascendancy over his mother and his word had become law. He guessed that she was afraid of him; perhaps even more afraid than she had been of Walter Brown, though he never resorted to violence with her; there was no need.

It was on their return from the cemetery that he issued

an edict: there were to be no more men to follow in the line of Brown and his predecessors.

'That's all finished and done with. From now on you sleep alone.'

She accepted the ban without protest. She was subdued and spiritless. 'Yes, Duggie. Anything you say.'

Only once did she break the rule and bring a man back to the house. It was someone she had picked up at the Blackamoor's Head, which she had started frequenting again now and then. The man was about fifty; he was bald-headed and wore glasses and had narrow shoulders and a pronounced stoop. He looked seedy, like a clerk who had fallen on bad times.

'Who are you?' Heeney asked.

It was Mrs Heeney who answered, nervously, looking anxiously and a shade apprehensively at her son. 'This is Mr Williams, a friend.' She turned to the man. 'My son, Douglas.'

Mr Williams smiled ingratiatingly and offered a bony hand. 'Pleased to meet you, Douglas.'

Heeney ignored the hand. 'Get out,' he said.

Mr Williams was taken aback. 'What?'

'I said get out. Piss off.'

There was no way Mr Williams could mistake Heeney's meaning; but he was not so easily dismissed. The reception was obviously not quite what he had expected, and he reacted by becoming very stiff and starchy, drawing himself up and pulling back his narrow shoulders as far as this was physically possible.

'Now look here, son –'

'I'm not your son,' Heeney said. 'Beat it.'

'Who are you to tell me what to do?' Williams demanded. 'I was invited in by the good lady your mother. Isn't that so, Norah?'

Heeney glanced at his mother. 'Oh, so it's Norah he calls you, is it? How long have you known this skinny old geezer?'

'Now, Duggie, please,' Mrs Heeney said. She looked at her son pleadingly. 'Be a good boy.'

'You should watch your tongue, too,' Mr Williams said reprovingly. 'You go round calling people names and you could find yourself in trouble.'

'Trouble from you?' Heeney spoke contemptuously. 'You couldn't make trouble for a three-year-old kid. Now are you going or aren't you?'

'No,' Williams said, 'I certainly am not. I never heard of such a thing. Being ordered about by a chit of a boy. What next?'

'Okay,' Heeney said. 'If you want to play it the hard way, so be it.'

He turned and walked into the back kitchen, only to return a moment later with a well-worn carving-knife.

Mrs Heeney uttered a scream. 'Oh no, Duggie! Don't! Please!'

Mr Williams stared at the knife and his jaw sagged a little. 'Now hold it, son.'

'I am holding it,' Heeney said. 'Are you going or do I have to see if there's any blood in that dried-up old carcase of yours?'

Mr Williams glanced at Mrs Heeney. 'He's mad. You never told me your son was crazy. He should be locked up. He's not safe to be out and about.'

Heeney made a thrust at him with the knife, and Williams did a backward jump to avoid the point.

'Now are you going to beat it? Next time I'll really puncture you, and that's a promise.'

Mr Williams's courage, such as it was, evaporated. He opened the street door and beat it.

Heeney put the knife down on the table. Mrs Heeney had slumped into her usual fireside chair and was crying. Heeney gave her a not very loving pat on the shoulder.

'Now don't be stupid; there's nothing to go on about. I told you before: no men. I told you, didn't I?'

'I didn't think you really meant it.'

'Well, now you know.'

She sniffed. 'You're very hard on me, Duggie.'

'Somebody's got to be. You want another experience like you had with Walter?'

'Mr Williams isn't like that. He's such a nice kind man. So well-mannered.'

'So they all are – to start with. Later on they turn into proper bastards.'

'Mr Williams wouldn't. He's different. He wouldn't ever get nasty.'

'He won't have the chance. You bring him back here again and I'll really carve him up. And any other man you fancy getting hooked up with. I'm not kidding, you know.'

She believed him; she knew he would use the knife if necessary. He intended having his own way and there was nothing she could do about it.

'I don't know what's got into you these days,' she said. 'You're getting to be a regular little tyrant. Ain't I allowed to have a life of my own.'

'You can have a life of your own as long as you stick to the rules. I'm not stopping you going to the pub and having a drink if that's what you want. But you don't bring any man back here. Never. You got that?'

She nodded dumbly.

'That's settled then.'

And it was.

Douglas Heeney was eighteen years old when a man picked him up outside the amusement arcade on Wharton Street. The man was driving a Jaguar car and he pulled it up to the kerb where Heeney was standing and asked him if he would like to go for a ride.

Heeney knew what this meant because it had happened before with other men, and if he had been flush he might have told this one to get stuffed; but he had thrown away his last coin on the machines in the arcade and was skint; so he accepted the offer and got into the car. It was a way of pulling in some easy money, even if it was not a way he favoured when there was any immediate alternative.

'My name's Humphrey,' the man said. He was a plump sleek person with rather long black hair, a smoothly shaven face and full moist lips. He was casually dressed in a fairly eye-catching outfit that included a flowered open-necked shirt, a purple velvet jacket, cream trousers and slip-on shoes with silver buckles. His hands on the steering-wheel were nicely manicured and there were rings on the fingers. In the lobe of one ear was a small gold star with a diamond in the centre. 'What do I call you, dear boy?'

'I'm Douglas,' Heeney said.

Humphrey took the Jaguar smoothly away from the kerb and slotted it into the traffic with practised skill. 'Well now, Douglas,' he said, 'is there anywhere in particular you'd like me to take you?'

'It's all the same to me,' Heeney said. 'You're the one that's driving.' The question was pointless anyway; the man would call the tune because he was the one that was going to pay the piper; they both knew that.

Humphrey chattered away as he drove and Heeney answered briefly or not at all. He soon realised that they were heading towards Rowton Park and one of the classier residential areas. Eventually they came to a tree-lined road where the large houses stood well back in their own grounds. Humphrey took the car in through the entrance to one of these properties and up a pebbled drive to the front of a weathered old house with creeper growing over the walls. He stopped there and switched off the engine.

'This your place?' Heeney asked, though he could guess the answer.

Humphrey smiled. 'Yes, it's my place. I thought

perhaps you might care to come inside and look at my paintings. What do you say to that?'

It sounded corny to Heeney, but what difference did it make? 'Yeah, if you like.'

Humphrey unlocked the panelled oak front door and ushered Heeney inside. There was a tiled entrance hall with the kind of gear that Heeney associated with antique dealers' shops – a brass-faced long-case clock, old oak chests, a mercury barometer, a scattering of rugs, some upright wooden chairs that looked wretchedly uncomfortable...

'Anyone else at home?'

'No,' Humphrey said. 'There's a cleaning woman who comes in daily, but she'll have left some time ago. We have the place all to ourselves.'

It was about what Heeney had expected; it was hardly likely that Humphrey would have brought him to meet his relations. What surprised him was that there really were paintings, genuine oils on canvas; it had not been just a line. They were at the back of the house on the second floor where some attics had been converted into a spacious studio with a wide expanse of glass on the north side. There were pictures everywhere, easels, a table cluttered with paints and pallettes and brushes in jars and all the other paraphernalia of the practising artist.

Humphrey appeared amused at Heeney's reaction. 'You thought I was kidding, didn't you, dear boy?'

Heeney stared at everything; it was an entirely new world to him; he had never been in a painter's studio before, had never even paused to consider the way in which works of art came to be produced.

'This is what you do? For a living?'

'For a living? Well, it could be if it were necessary. And I do sell them now and then. There are two in the Wakeham Gallery. You may have seen them.'

'No,' Heeney said. He knew the Wakeham Gallery,

that mid-Victorian building in the classic style which stood not more than a hundred yards from Haig Street Station, only from the outside; he had never set foot inside its walls; it was not the kind of place to which his mother would have been likely to take him. 'I don't know much about that sort of thing. Never thought about it really.'

Humphrey appeared unsurprised; it was probably what he had expected. There were some unframed canvases stacked against a wall, and he picked them up one by one, placing each in turn on an easel for Heeney to see. Several of them were paintings of nudes, all male, boys or young men, in various poses, skilfully, even perhaps lovingly, executed.

'What do you think of them?'

Heeney was unimpressed; he would have got more pleasure from looking at female nudes; these failed to excite him. But Humphrey apparently specialised in the male figure. Which was maybe only to be expected.

'They're all right, I reckon. I don't know nothing about art.'

'It's a gap in your education. Perhaps we can do something about that. How would you like to sit for me one of these days?'

'Oh, I don't know.' Heeney was not exactly drawn to the idea; he was not sure he wanted to have himself so revealingly portrayed on canvas for anyone to look at. In fact he was pretty damned sure he did not.

'I would pay you for it, of course. The model is worthy of his hire, eh?'

That certainly made a difference, but Heeney doubted whether the pay would be enough to compensate for the indignity. And suppose somebody he knew ever got to see the picture. He would never live it down.

'Well,' Humphrey said, 'no need to make up your mind straightaway. Think about it.'

'Okay.'

Humphrey cooked an evening meal in a kitchen that was like something out of the glossy women's magazines that Heeney's mother got hold of now and then; it was all bright and gleaming, with every kind of gadget you could think of. It was pretty obvious that the painter rather prided himself on his cookery. Heeney watched him at it, while Humphrey kept up a running commentary on what he was doing; he was a great talker and occasionally he would put a hand on Heeney's arm and call him 'dear boy'.

Whenever Humphrey touched him Heeney wanted to give him a knee in the groin, but he had to behave himself for the present at least. Later he might do something about it, but not now.

He was not much impressed by the meal which finally resulted from all the elaborate preparation; it might have been cordon bleu cookery but it was not to his taste; he would rather have had a helping of fish-and-chips wrapped in paper and eaten with fingers for forks. Humphrey must have noticed that he did not exactly relish the food, and it was probably a big disappointment to him after he had employed all his culinary skills in order to please his young guest.

He gave a sad little shake of the head. 'I fear we shall have to educate you in the appreciation of good food also, dear boy.'

Heeney could have told him that there would be no education for him either in art or the pleasures of the table, because he had no intention of becoming a pupil in these subjects; but he let it pass.

He was happier with the bathroom; he had never seen one quite so sumptuous; it was a long way from the tin bath in front of the kitchen range at home. The bath was enormous, let into the floor so that you just stepped down into it; and there was plenty of room for Humphrey to share it with him. Water came out of a gold-plated mixer tap in the pink-tiled wall and there was some liquid squeezed out of a polythene bottle which made a froth on the surface like the foam whipped up by waves falling on a sandy beach. The cake of soap was the size of an ostrich's egg and smelled like the inside of a tart's handbag.

What disgusted Heeney was the sight of Humphrey's naked body; it was so soft and smooth and flabby, in stark contrast to his own lean and bony frame which all too obviously excited the artist. Heeney detested Humphrey's pawing, but he had to endure it, had to keep telling himself to be patient, even when he felt like spitting in the man's face.

When they had dried themselves Humphrey gave his guest a silk dressing-gown to wear and draped himself in another. They then went to a room furnished in a kind of oriental style and reclined on softly-cushioned settees, smoking Turkish cigarettes and drinking champagne.

Heeney was none too keen on the champagne; he disliked all bubbly drinks and he failed to see why people were so crazy about the stuff. He let Humphrey do most of the drinking and took only a sip or two now and then for himself. He was hoping the wine would act as a sleeping-draught and make the man drowsy, and eventually it did seem to have that effect. Humphrey began to yawn and suggested that it was time for bed.

'If that suits you, dear boy.'

'Okay,' Heeney said. 'Let's get it over with.'

SIX
Promise

It was coming up to three o'clock in the morning when Heeney slipped carefully out of the bed and switched on a heavily shaded bedside lamp. Humphrey was lying on his side with his head half-buried in a pillow, and he was making faint snoring noises. It was evident that he was sound asleep, and he did not move while Heeney quickly dressed himself.

'I ought to smother you, you fat bastard,' Heeney muttered. It would be easy; all he had to do was take a pillow and hold it down on Humphrey's head until the life in him expired. It would be no loss either, because slobs like him were trash, filthy perverts who did not deserve to live. It did not occur to him to ask the question: if Humphrey was trash, what was he? What was the parasite that sucked the blood of this trash?

Heeney did not carry his mental processes that far; he just knew that he hated the man he was making use of, hated him so fiercely that the desire to kill him was almost irresistible. But he did resist it, simply because it was in his own interest to do so; and always with him his own interest came first. Alive, he knew that Humphrey would never be any threat to him, would never take any action because the publicity would be so damaging to his own reputation. But a dead Humphrey would inevitably bring in the police, and once they got their noses into

59

the business there was no telling what might happen.

'Bastard!' he muttered again, and turned away from the bed.

He found the soft leather note-case in a pocket of Humphrey's jacket. There was a thick wad of paper money inside it, which he did not bother to count but stuffed into his own pocket. There was a gold cigarette-case also and he took that, too. He switched off the lamp and groped his way to the door, letting himself silently out of the room and closing the door gently behind him.

He found a switch and snapped it on, illuminating the landing and the stairs. He was about to descend to the hall when an idea occurred to him, and instead of going down he went up to the attic studio and switched the light on in there. Working quickly he took the paintings of the nude young men and laid them face upward on the floor. There were tubes of paint lying on the table and he squeezed the contents of these on to the canvases before taking up a handful of brushes and smearing the paint all over the portraits until they were completely obliterated in a mess of garish colour.

'That for you, Mr Humphrey!' he snarled. 'That for you, you bloody queer!'

To vent even more his loathing of the man he had an urge to dance on the pictures, to smash them completely; but it would have entailed getting paint on his shoes and he restrained himself.

He switched the light off before leaving the studio and went silently down the heavily carpeted stairs. There was no sound coming from the room where Humphrey was blissfully sleeping off the effects of the champagne, oblivious of the act of vandalism that had been perpetrated on the floor above.

Heeney crossed the tiled hall and let himself out of the house just as a faint grey light was beginning to make itself apparent in the eastern sky.

*

He was walking along Cawston Road when a police car came up behind and stopped by the kerb a few yards ahead of him. He had a crazy impulse to turn and run, but it would have been the worst thing he could have done, so he just walked on. When he drew level with the police car he could see that the nearside window was down and that a uniformed constable had his head poking out. There was another uniformed man in the driving seat.

'Hey, you there!' the one at the window called out. 'Just a minute!'

Heeney stopped. 'You talking to me?'

'That's right,' the policeman said. 'Where are you going, son?'

'Home.'

'Where's that?'

'Marshall Street,' Heeney said. It was nowhere near where he lived.

'That's a long way from here.'

'Yes, it is.'

'Where've you been?'

'With a pal. We was playing cards at his house.'

'Till this hour?'

'We must've fell asleep. When I woke up it was past three.'

'So then you came away?'

'Yes.'

'You should've stayed for breakfast.'

'No; I had to get home. It's on account of my old ma, see? She don't know where I am and she'll be worrying.'

It sounded thin and he doubted whether they believed him, because coppers were suspicious by nature and always inclined to think you were lying to them. So they might decide to give him a body search, and then they would find the money and the cigarette-case. He might explain away the cash but never the solid gold fag-case; so maybe it would be best to run before they got to work on him; he might lose them among the houses if they had to follow on foot.

'What's your name, son?'

'Alec Smith,' he said.

'I hope you're not a smart Alec,' the policeman said.

Heeney said nothing.

The policeman treated him to a long hard look and must have come to the conclusion that he was not worth bothering about. Maybe it was getting near the end of his spell of duty and he wanted no extra work.

'Okay, Alec. On your way.'

Heeney started walking, though he felt more inclined to break into a run, and the police car drove off and disappeared in the distance.

'Filthy swine!' Heeney muttered. But it could have been a lot worse; he could have been arrested.

Even then he did not go straight home; instead he made his way to the place of business of Mr Alfred Waite. The yard at the rear of Waite's shop was closed by a tall wooden gate and at this hour in the morning the gate was padlocked. For one as young and agile as Heeney, however, this was no great obstacle, and having cast a quick glance to left and right to make sure he was unobserved, he made a jump, got a fingerhold on the top of the gate and hauled himself up and over.

The yard was in semi-darkness, but he found his way to the back door and started ringing the bell. For some time there was no response, but he kept at it and eventually he saw a light come on behind an upstairs window. Soon after that there was a sound of bolts being slid back and the door opened an inch or two to reveal Alfred Waite's hollow-cheeked face in the gap.

'What is it?' he demanded in a peevish voice. 'What do you want?'

'It's me, Duggie,' Heeney said. 'I got something for you.'

'Go away,' Waite said. 'Come back some other time.' He

made a move to close the door.

Heeney stuck a foot in the gap and prevented the closure. 'No, it's gotta be now. None of your games.'

Waite reluctantly agreed to let him in. 'But you'll have to shift your foot, else I can't get the chain off.'

'All right, but don't try bolting it on me or I'll stand here and ring the bell for as long as it takes.'

He withdrew his foot and Waite released the chain, mumbling complaints all the time. Heeney walked in and the pawnbroker secured the door. They were in a narrow lobby illuminated by a low-power electric bulb. Waite was in pyjamas and a shabby old dressing-gown, his feet thrust into frayed carpet-slippers.

'You better come in here,' he said, and he led the way into the junk-cluttered room where Heeney had done business with him on many previous occasions.

'Well, what have you got?' he asked. 'It'd better be good, getting me out of bed at this time in the morning like I was open all hours of the day and night.'

Heeney produced the cigarette-case. 'This.'

Waite took it in his skinny fingers and examined it closely. 'What else?'

'Nothing else,' Heeney said.

'You got me up just for this?'

'It's something, ain't it? It's solid gold and heavy. There's a hallmark on it.'

'What do you know about hallmarks?' Waite was scathing. 'You wouldn't know one mark from another.'

'Are you telling me it's not gold?'

'Maybe it is, maybe not.'

'Come off it,' Heeney said. 'You know damn well it is.' He felt pretty certain a man like Humphrey would have nothing but the genuine article; you just had to look at the rest of the things in his house to know that he only went for the best. No rolled gold for him.

'It's got a monogram on it,' Waite said. 'HBJ. Who's this HBJ?'

'Never mind,' Heeney said. 'What's the odds? The monogram won't be there when it's been melted down.'

'Two quid,' Waite said.

'Two quid!' Heeney was indignant. 'Two miserable bloody quid! It's worth more than that.'

'So it may be. But not to me. If you don't like the price you can go and try somewhere else. See what Maples on Blyth Street will give you.'

'Don't talk daft,' Heeney said. Maples was a high-class jeweller's shop in one of the more select parts of the town. 'I can't go there; you know I can't.'

Alfred Waite gave a histrionic shrug which brought his shoulders up round his ears. 'That's your problem.'

'You could at least make it five. That wouldn't be asking much.'

'And make no profit for myself? How long would I stay in business if I went along those lines?'

Eventually Heeney managed to squeeze an extra fifty pence out of him. It was robbery: he had robbed Humphrey and now Waite was robbing him. But he had to take what he could get; he could never have used the cigarette-case for himself, that was for sure.

Waite accompanied him across the yard and unlocked the gate; it was much lighter now and there was a risk that somebody might see Heeney if he were to climb over it again, and that would draw unwanted attention to the place.

On his way back to his mother's house Heeney reflected that Alfred Waite was a thieving old skinflint and that it might be advisable to look for some alternative market for the merchandise he acquired. Unfortunately, it was not so easy to find a good fence; you had to be careful how you went about the job of looking for one or you could be in real trouble. So maybe for the present he would have to stick to Waite, stingy as the old bastard might be. But some day things would be different; some day he would move into a bigger league where there were richer rewards. He had to look to the future.

His mother was still in bed when he arrived home, and he let himself into the house. The first thing he did was to count the money he had taken from Humphrey's note-case. There was more than he had imagined; altogether it added up to one hundred and forty-five pounds. Well, that was not bad, not bad at all. And when it came to the point money was best; you had no need to go to a fence with that kind of take, and it was worth its full value, too; nobody else took a percentage. Oh, sure, there was a lot to be said for money.

He peeled off twenty pounds and put the notes under a vase on the mantelpiece, stowing the rest of them back in his pocket. The fire in the grate had burned low and the room was chilly. He debated in his mind whether or not to go to bed, but it was past five o'clock and he decided not to. He got the fire going again and sat down in the armchair which his mother usually occupied. He was asleep when she came into the room, and it was the sound of her drawing back the curtains that woke him.

'Hullo, Ma,' he said. 'So you're up.'

She swung round. 'My!' she exclaimed. 'You didn't half give me a start. I never saw you sitting there. When'd you come in?'

'Late.'

'Why didn't you go to bed?'

'Oh, I sat down for a minute and I must've dropped off.'

It was broad daylight now, and the fire had died down again. Mrs Heeney was in the grubby old dressing-gown which she usually wore for half the morning; on her feet she had a pair of mangy-looking fur-trimmed mules which made a flip-flopping sound as she walked. Her face was a mess.

'Where you been?' she asked.

'Never you mind,' Heeney said. He had no intention

of telling her about Humphrey. She would have been shocked; and the less she knew about his activities the less she could tell anyone else if they ever questioned her.

He got up from the chair, yawned and stretched himself. 'There's some money for you.' He pointed at the notes under the vase on the mantelpiece.

She went flip-flopping across to the fireplace and took the cash. 'Twenty quid! Where'd you get this?'

'I won it.'

'You always was a lucky boy.'

'Luck don't come into it,' Heeney said.

She gave him a slightly anxious look. 'You wouldn't be getting into no trouble, would you, Duggie?'

'Course not. What trouble would I be getting into?'

'I don't know. I just wish you had a steady job.'

'Where would I find a steady job in this run-down has-been of a town?'

'There must be something.'

'Not for me, there ain't.'

'Have you tried?'

'What do you think?'

'I don't know what to think. I worry about you; I reely worry about you, Dug.'

Heeney grinned at her. 'Don't keep you awake nights, does it? Look, Ma, I'll get by. There's no need for you to bother yourself about me. I can look after myself.'

'Well,' she said doubtfully, 'just so long as you don't go getting into trouble…'

Trouble, he thought; that was what she was always on about. And maybe she had had enough of it in her time to make her want no more; maybe all she asked for from now on was a quiet life. And where did that get you in the end? Into a cold hole in the ground in some graveyard or a hot oven in a crematorium. Himself, he wanted more than that, a lot more. And he was never going to get it by looking for a steady job; all that did for you was wear out the soles of your shoes.

He put a hand on his mother's shoulder. 'No trouble, Ma.'

She looked at him. 'Promise?'

'Promise.'

SEVEN
Odd

Sometimes Heeney wondered how much his mother guessed regarding his activities. She asked very few questions because he always choked her off when she did. Eventually she came to realise that she would get nothing out of him and she no longer tried. But she must have been suspicious, because although he had no job he never drew any dole money, and in fact had never made any attempt to milk the Social Security system; yet he rarely seemed to be short of cash and often gave her some to help with the housekeeping.

So where did it come from?

His story was always the same: he had won it, at cards or on the dogs or maybe even a horse. It was possible that she accepted this as the truth, but he doubted it; she could not be that dumb. But it made no difference, one way or the other.

And in fact sometimes it really was the truth; he went to the greyhound racing stadium fairly often, and now and then he won a decent amount. But he was not a compulsive gambler and looked upon that sort of occupation as a mug's game. Betting occasionally on the dogs was just a bit of relaxation, as was the infrequent visit to a betting shop to put a pound or two on the horses; but he was no student of form and was contemptuous of those who professed to make a scientific assessment of the runners. They lost as often as those who relied on the closed eyes and the pin.

Meanwhile he was making a living from petty thievery and still using the services of Alfred Waite as a fence simply because he had been unable to find a better market for his wares. And because he was a fairly regular supplier and knew the kind of objects that were most saleable Waite had become a shade more generous with the payment. It was possible that the crooked pawnbroker recognised the value of his client and had no wish to run the risk of losing him.

So Heeney followed his chosen trade of entering houses to which he had not been invited and pocketing whatever of value came easily to hand; and time passed and he came up to his twenty-first birthday without ever having been caught in this nefarious occupation. He had had a few scares of course; sometimes a householder would awake when he should have remained asleep and Heeney would be forced to make a quick getaway, but he was always careful after having forced an entry to leave an easy way of retreat, and he made a practice of wearing close-fitting black leather gloves in order not to leave any incriminating fingerprints.

And then, less than a week after his twenty-first birthday, an incident occurred which made a complete change in his routine and set him off on a very different track. The house was in one of those middle-class residential areas of Seaport which were his most productive hunting-grounds. It was detached, surrounded by a fair-sized garden, with a stretch of lawn in front and a gravel drive. It was one o'clock in the morning and there was a not a light showing.

Heeney took a quick look up and down the road to make sure no one was around and then opened the gate in the low wall which enclosed the property. Once inside he got himself on to the grass and walked soft-footed up to the house which was faintly visible as a kind of deeper darkness in the gloom. He was alert for any indication that there might be a dog anywhere around, for dogs were the devil, even if they were only of the small yappy variety, and the least sign of one was always sufficient to make him give up any idea of breaking and entering straightaway.

But no such animal gave a hint of its presence on this occasion, and he left the lawn and made his way round to the rear of the house. Here there was a glazed sun-porch or conservatory which had probably been added a good many years after the erection of the original building, and there was a concrete patio with some small shrubs in tubs dotted around and a wooden seat.

Heeney tried the door on the sun-porch and found that it was locked. He never carried any house-breaking tools with him, because if you were stopped by a policeman and found to be carrying a jemmy or anything of that description you were likely to be arrested on the spot. For a similar reason he only took away with him small objects like jewellery and watches which he could slip into his pockets, since any man walking around with a bag or suitcase in the middle of the night was bound to be regarded with suspicion.

Quite frequently he would find a door left unlocked or a downstairs window slightly open, especially when the householder had been doing a decorating job and wanted the paint to harden. And even if every door and window was secured you could often find a tool in the garden shed or some such place to use for breaking in. An ordinary spade was as good as a jemmy; you could slip the blade in between the door and the jamb and get a lot of leverage with the handle. It took a very strong lock to stand up to that kind of treatment.

In the present instance there were no doors or windows unfastened and no handy tools lying around, so he returned to the sun-porch and put his gloved fist through the pane of glass nearest to the lock on the door. The splinters of glass fell on to a mat on the inside and made no more than a faint tinkling sound and he removed the pieces still clinging to the frame. Reaching with his hand through the hole he found to his delight that the key had been left in the lock. It never ceased to amaze him that, despite all the warnings, there were still thousands of people as careless as ever with their security arrangements. Which was lucky for operators like him, since it made life a whole lot easier.

He unlocked the door and let himself into the sun-porch, which was so cluttered with gear that he had to be very careful not to knock anything over in the darkness. He had a small pocket torch with him, and now he took it out and switched it on. The light revealed that there was an inner door which was actually standing ajar, and a moment later he was in the kitchen.

Quickly but methodically he went from room to room on the ground floor, making a rapid search for any small objects of value that he might carry away; but though the furnishing gave evidence of considerable affluence he found nothing to his purpose. Disappointed at this level, he decided to try the first floor, knowing from experience that bedrooms often provided richer pickings than the rooms below. He had purloined many articles of jewellery as well as ready money from pockets or purses while their owners slept on undisturbed, perhaps only a few feet away.

Climbing the staircase he made no sound on the soft pile of the carpet, and he reached the landing and opened the first door he came to. Two of the bedrooms proved unproductive; they had the look of chambers that were not currently in use and he wasted little time on them. The third was larger, and he would have known simply by the odour that it was occupied by a woman. But a quick glance at the big double bed illuminated by the small beam of the pocket torch revealed no head on the pillow, and he turned his atten- ion to the dressing-table.

Here there was more to reward him: a gold bangle, a pair of ear-rings, a necklace, lying there just as a woman might have laid them carelessly down before undressing. Heeney began to stow them in this pocket, and he had the necklace in his hand when he heard a faint click and a bedside lamp came on.

He swung round and saw that he had been too cursory in his inspection of the bed; there had been someone in it and that someone was a woman. She must have been snuggled under the duvet, and though he had made very little sound it had obviously been enough to waken her. Now she was sitting up in the bed, holding the duvet up to her throat and staring at him where he stood by the dressing-table with the necklace in one hand and the torch in the other.

'Now what,' she said, 'do you think you're doing in my bedroom?'

And the surprising thing was that she seemed quite calm and did not sound at all alarmed to discover a strange man standing by her dressing-table in the small hours of the morning. She should have been scared out of her wits, but she was not; and it took Heeney out of his stride, so that for the moment he could think of nothing to say and just stood there staring back at the woman.

He saw that she had long dark brown hair and she raised the hand that was not clutching the duvet and combed it back from her forehead with her fingers. He made a guess that she was approaching the forty mark in years, if she had not already passed it, but she had not lost her looks and must have been a real beauty when younger.

'Well,' she said, 'how much longer are you going to stand there as dumb as a post? You haven't lost your tongue, have you?'

'No,' Heeney said.

'Is that all you have to say for yourself?'

'What do you expect me to say?'

'You might begin by telling me what you're doing with my necklace.'

Heeney looked at the necklace in his hand and put it back on the dressing-table. He also switched off the torch and put it in his pocket. But he was still not sure what else to do; the situation was quite unlike any other he had found himself in; the coolness of the woman put him at a disadvantage.

She was still looking at him curiously. 'You're very young, aren't you? Isn't there some better way for a nice-looking boy like you to pick up a living?'

'Well –' Heeney said. But there was really nothing he could say in answer to that sort of question and he fell silent again.

The woman beckoned to him with her free hand. 'Come over here where I can see you better.'

Heeney hesitated for a moment and then walked over to the bed. At close quarters the woman was still worth a second glance, and maybe more than that. Heeney looked down at her bare arms and shoulders and had an impulse to reach out and touch them. He could see the hollow where her neck came down towards the collar-bone and he felt a stirring of sexual desire.

She seemed to guess what was in his mind and she gave a little laugh. 'Don't tell me you're thinking of raping me now.'

He made no reply; for of course the thought had been there, though he might scarcely have been aware of it himself; not in plain words.

She laughed again, with a kind of gurgle in the throat. 'Forget it. There's no need, is there?' With a sudden movement of the hand she thrust the duvet aside and revealed that under the covering she was completely nude.

His pulse raced as he stared at her. What was she? Some kind of nympho? Because there could be no doubt that she was quite blatantly offering herself to him. It was as though she had been waiting for someone like him to come to her and was glad that he was there.

And there could be no doubt either that he wanted to accept the offer. Lying half on her side and half on her back in the soft warm bed, there was a voluptuousness about her that was irresistible. It choked him and he was dumb again, sweating a little.

'So what are you waiting for?' she asked. 'Why don't you get yourself out of those damned clothes and come to bed?'

It was, Heeney thought, all a question of class. That was what made the difference between her and the others he had been with. This woman had class and they had had none; and it mattered nothing that she was old enough to have been his mother, nothing at all.

Her name was Fenella and she was a divorcee; that much she told him about herself but little more. It was evident that she had money, and he wondered why she had not married again; it should have been easy for a woman with her physical attractions to have found a second husband. But perhaps in her case once was enough; perhaps she enjoyed the freedom of being single.

She got him talking about himself, and she seemed really interested. Perhaps he ought not to have told her so much, ought to have kept a lock on his tongue. But maybe it was because she was so much older that he found himself confiding in her, trusting her. And there was that aura of class about her, too; it did surely make all the difference.

'Tell me,' she said, 'how did you get into the house? I'm sure I locked the doors.'

He told her.

'As easy as that!'

'As easy as that. You oughter be more careful. Anyone could've got in.'

It seemed to amuse her that he of all people should be giving her a lecture on security. And he could see the oddity in it himself.

'And you do this all the time?' she asked. 'Breaking into houses and taking whatever you find lying around.'

'Only if it's small and valuable. That's very important. I don't go for junk.'

'Ah, I see you're a connoisseur.'

He detected a chaffing note and answered sulkily: 'I know what's what.'

'Oh, I'm sure you do. And this is a living?'

'I get by.'

'But doesn't it ever occur to you that there might be better ways for someone as clever as you to make his way in life? Haven't you thought of that?'

'Yes, I have,' he said. 'Some day I'll make a change.'

She had touched a nerve with her question; he had indeed thought about it, but not quite as she had meant. His idea of a better way was as illegal as the present one. But he did not tell her so.

She stroked his cheek. 'You do that, Douglas. I'd hate to think of you wasting your talents.'

He wondered whether she was chaffing him again; with her it was difficult to tell. He drew away from her.

'I gotta go. It's getting late.'

'It was late when you came,' she said. But she made no attempt to detain him.

He dressed quickly. She pulled the duvet over her and lay there watching him. When he started moving towards the door she said:

'Aren't you forgetting something?'

He stopped. 'Forgetting what?'

'The necklace.'

'Oh, that. Well –' He hesitated, then gave a shrug,

walked to the dressing-table and put the necklace in his pocket with the bangle and the ear-rings.

Again he was moving away and again she stopped him. 'You haven't looked inside that lacquer box. Why don't you?'

He saw the box she was referring to and opened it. Inside were some more pieces of jewellery: a diamond clasp, another pair of ear-rings, an emerald on a fine gold chain, rings... He could not understand why she had told him about them when she could see that he had been leaving; but if she was crazy enough to do so, why should he worry? He scooped up the jewels and stowed them away with the other items he had already pocketed.

This time she said nothing as he walked to the door, just lay in the bed, following his movements with her eyes. She was an odd one, he thought; she really was.

He was halfway down the stairs when a suspicion hit him like a blow, bringing him to a dead stop. She had been fooling him; that was the truth of it. He remembered the telephone on the bedside table. Suppose right now she was calling the police! Suppose when he got out there in the road he found himself being chased by a patrol car! He had the jewels on him; the jewels she had practically begged him to take. And suppose she brought a charge of rape against him, identified him as the man who had broken in, assaulted her and stolen her jewellery! He would be in it then, up to the neck.

He turned and raced back up the stairs. When he entered the bedroom she had the telephone in her hand and was dialling a number. So he had been right, dead bloody right. All that sweet talk she had given him, all that hugging and kissing, had been nothing but a part of the trap laid for him to fall into. And he had taken the bait and walked into the trap with his eyes open, thinking she really liked him; her with her class! He must be going soft in the head.

'You bitch!' he said.

She had stopped dialling and was staring at him with the telephone in her hand. And this time she did look scared; it showed in her eyes. And she had reason to look like that, damned good reason; because he was in a rage. She had fooled him and he hated her for it. She had got him to talk about himself and he had believed she was sympathetic, while all the time she was just laughing at him, leading him on.

'You bitch!' he said again. 'You were calling the coppers.'

'No,' she said.

'Who, then?'

'A friend, just a friend.'

'At this time of night! You expect me to believe that?'

'It's the truth. I swear it is.'

He hit her on the side of the face with his gloved fist. She dropped the telephone and a trickle of blood appeared at the corner of her mouth.

'Don't,' she said. 'Don't hurt me. Please. I'll give you anything, do anything you ask. But please don't hurt me.'

'You've done enough,' Heeney said. 'You've done too bloody much, you cow.' And he hit her again, on the other side of the face.

She began to moan. He picked up one of the pillows and covered her head with it, pressing it down and holding it there so that she could not breathe. She struggled violently at first, but he was too strong for her and kept the pillow crushed down on her face until she ceased to move.

Even then he did not at once remove the pillow but held it down while the minutes ticked by, making sure, making absolutely sure that the spark of life had been finally extinguished.

Then he replaced the telephone receiver on its cradle and took the jewellery from his pocket and made a little heap of it on the dressing-table. It might have been safe to keep it, but there was a risk and he never took unnecessary risks.

He switched off the bedside lamp and guided himself out of the house with the pocket torch. Reason told him that it had been a bad night's work, and yet the overriding feeling was one of elation which seemed to give a spring to his step as he walked away down the road.

It was odd, that.

Yet, after all, she might have been telling the truth; she might have been ringing a friend who happened to be an insomniac. Maybe she had really taken a liking to him and had wanted him to keep the jewellery as a gift. Maybe.

But he could never have been certain of it and it would have been crazy to take a gamble on the possibility.

Nevertheless, it really was all very odd; especially that sense of elation which was putting the spring in his step.

EIGHT

Cache

The encounter with the woman named Fenella marked a turning-point in Heeney's criminal career. It was the last house-breaking job he did. After that he had no more dealings with Alfred Waite and never again went near the pawnbroker's shop. He had come to the end of one phase of his life and was starting on another.

He had struck up an acquaintanceship with a man named Snappy Deacon. Snappy was a nickname he had been given because of a habit he had of using his teeth in fights; it was said that he had once bitten off a man's ear in a pub brawl, but Heeney was not sure whether this was true or not. Deacon himself had never mentioned it.

The two men had run across each other at the Boundary Greyhound Stadium, and it was not until much later that Heeney realised that the meeting had not been entirely fortuitous. The fact was that Snappy Deacon had had an eye on him for some time and had made some discreet inquiries regarding Heeney's background. For Deacon was on the look-out for a suitable candidate to fill a vacancy and he had come to the conclusion that Heeney was likely material.

Deacon was rather like a scout for a football club or a headhunter in the world of big business; the difference was that he was looking for somewhat less socially acceptable qualities in his man; qualities which most people might in fact have regarded as precisely the opposite. He was a good judge of character and it had not taken him long to arrive at a pretty accurate assessment of Heeney's rating in that respect.

One evening as the two men were taking some refreshment together in the restaurant at the stadium Deacon broached the subject which had been uppermost in his mind for quite some time.

'How,' he said, 'would you like to earn some easy money?'

Heeney looked at him warily. Deacon was a chunky sort of person who had a curious weakness for blue double-breasted suits that were slightly too small for him, so that you could see his muscles bulging here and there. He had closely cropped fair hair which was beginning to reveal a circle of bare scalp on the top of his skull and there was a bit of scar tissue on each eyebrow. He had, so he told Heeney, once been in the prize-fighting business as a middleweight but had given it up because he could see it was leading nowhere, except perhaps to a helping of brain damage and punch-drunkenness.

'What sort of amount are we talking about?' Heeney asked. 'Big or small?'

'Could be big.'

Heeney absorbed this information and asked for more. 'Would it be legal or illegal?'

Deacon grinned at him, showing a gap in his front teeth that might have been a memento of his pugilistic days. 'Would it bother you if it was illegal?'

'No,' Heeney said, 'it wouldn't bother me. Not as long as there was enough of the crackling to make it worth my while.'

'It'd be worth your while,' Deacon assured him. 'I can promise you that.'

The first job he did with the Roxy gang was a fairly minor

one: he acted as a look-out man while they broke into a warehouse and stole a vanload of fur coats. He was paid two hundred pounds for his trouble; which was hardly big money but was certainly easy. Deacon said it was just a start and there was no reason why he should not get a lot more in the future if he proved to be worth his salt.

With the addition of Heeney there were five of them in the Roxy gang. Joe Roxy, the leader, was a dapper black-haired man who had been an army quartermaster-sergeant but had been kicked out of the service as a result of certain dishonest practices designed to augment his normal pay. He was forty years old and was the brains of the outfit; he planned each operation with care and saw that it was carried out with military precision. He it was also who arranged the disposal of the loot, and in fact he never put the gang on to a job unless he had already lined up a buyer for what was going to be stolen. That way an immediate sale of the hot goods and a quick cash payment were assured.

The other two members of the gang were fairly run-of-the-mill villains, going by the names of Billy Wadkins and Jerry Mouncer; not very high in the IQ stakes but strong in the arm and capable of carrying out orders.

Joe Roxy had given Heeney a thorough going-over when Deacon introduced him; he was not the man to take anyone on trust. But in the end he seemed to be satisfied that Heeney would fit in.

'But remember this, son: I'm the boss. You do what I tell you and you do it right. Understand?'

'I understand,' Heeney said. 'You can count on me. I won't never let you down.'

'You better not,' Roxy said. 'And I hope you know how to keep a still tongue in your head.'

'I know.'

'Good. There's some just has to go blabbing around; can't keep things to theirselves. And then maybe someone as shouldn't gets to hear things and goes along to the cop he's working for and that's when the trouble starts. I wouldn't like to think you was a blabbermouth.'

When Roxy said this Heeney could almost feel his eyes boring into him, probing his mind. He got the impression that though Roxy was not a big man in the physical sense he would be a bad one to cross.

'I'm no blabbermouth,' he said. 'I'm an oyster.'

It was on his third job with the Roxy gang that Heeney distinguished himself in a small way. He slugged a storehouse watchman with a short length of lead pipe bound with insulating tape just as the man was about to raise the alarm. The watchman went out like a light, and Heeney tied him up and gagged him while the others went on loading a van with video recorders.

It earned him a word of praise from Joe Roxy himself. 'You done that real smart, Duggie. We could've had trouble, but you nipped it in the bud. You're handy with the cosh.'

Heeney shrugged. 'Somebody had to do him.'

'And you was the one that did. That's what I like, a man who can think quick and act quick. Snappy picked the right boy when he enlisted you.'

'Well, thanks,' Heeney said. 'I do my best.'

'You go on doing that and we shan't have no cause for complaint.'

Heeney was not sure he liked Roxy; there was a bit too much of the army NCO about him; handing out his orders and expecting everyone to jump smartly to it when he gave the word. Heeney had been used to being his own boss and going his own sweet way regardless of what anyone else might want him to do. Now all that had changed; he was one of a team and he had to do as he was told.

But the rewards were good; he was soon pulling in far more than that first hand-out of two hundred pounds;

and what he was getting now made the pickings that he had been getting from his house-breaking racket look very small beer indeed.

Nevertheless, he was still living with his mother, even though there were many nights when his bed at the terrace house was unused. Mrs Heeney seemed to guess that there had been a change in his mode of life, though he had told her nothing of his linking up with the Roxy gang. For that matter, he had never told her about his house-breaking exploits either, and she seldom asked any questions regarding his activities, probably reasoning that it might be better not to know too much.

Certainly if she had known that he had killed a woman she would have been worried sick; but he had never given her the slightest hint of that business. And though the murder had made headlines in the papers and she had read about it, there had been no reason at all why she should have connected him with the affair. The police had not done so, either; and this did not surprise him, for there had been nothing to point them in his direction. So after a while it became just one more of those cases which were left on the file but showed no sign of ever being solved.

Heeney was careful not to make any show with the money that was now coming to him in increasing quantity; he had no wish to draw attention to himself. But he had to stow the cash away somewhere, and without a bank account of any kind this presented something of a problem. He rejected the idea of hiding it in the house, because one could never rule out the possibility of a search of the premises being made if the police should come to have suspicions regarding him; and the discovery of a large sum of money secreted under the floorboards or sewn up in a mattress might give rise to speculation and awkward questions being asked.

The classic way of disposing of ill-gotten gains was of

course to open a numbered Swiss bank account; but he was not sure how to set about doing that, and he doubted whether the amount he had in hand would have been particularly interesting to any of the Gnomes of Zurich, who were used to dealing in millions rather than hundreds or even thousands.

In the end he bought a metal cash-box to hold the notes and buried it under the brick floor in a corner of the outside privy. He carried out this task at night, while his mother was in bed, and when he had finished the job the loose bricks resting on the box appeared indistinguishable from any of the others.

It was no more than a temporary measure; he had no intention of sticking with the Roxy lot indefinitely. Vague plans were forming in his mind for the day when he had amassed sufficient capital to put them into effect. Then he would break free from Roxy and Deacon and the others and go his own way. But it would not be for a while yet; a few more years maybe. He had to be patient.

Unfortunately, in his case patience had not been rewarded; fate had caught up with him in the shape of an officer named Roy Denver of the Seaport CID. There were other officers involved as well, but it was Denver on whom Heeney's considerable animosity was concentrated; for Denver had been in charge of the operation that had finally nailed the Roxy gang and put the members in jail for varying lengths of time.

It had happened when they were quietly helping themselves to a quantity of valuable office equipment – computers, word processors, copiers and the like. It was three o'clock in the morning and they had just started to load the van when a lot of policemen, plain-clothes and uniformed, had burst into the warehouse and started making arrests.

Heeney wished he had had a shooter, like maybe a pump-action shotgun. He would have used it. But Joe

Roxy had always made it a strict rule that none of the gang was to carry a firearm; he said guns made more trouble for you than they were worth; people got killed and then you really were in the filth. His aim was to plan everything so well that nothing could go wrong, and then there would be no need for lethal weapons of any kind.

But things did not always work out as planned even with clever Dicks like him in charge, and that last job certainly went off the rails good and proper. Somebody must surely have given the coppers a tip-off, because why else would they have been lying in wait all ready to make the nab? Heeney would have liked to know who it was who had grassed, but he had no idea. It could not have been one of the gang, because they were all arrested and all sent down for their part in the attempted robbery. So who had it been? It was a mystery.

Even without a shooter he had given a good account of himself, and they had not taken him easily. He had used the cosh to good effect, and two of the coppers had received injuries which had put them in hospital for a while. But the thought of something like that was small consolation when you were shut up in prison for a period of years.

During those years Heeney brooded much on the ill-fortune that had brought him to this pass. It never occurred to him to reflect that he was merely receiving the just punishment for his crimes, or that if he had had his full deserts he might have been serving a life sentence for the murder of a woman named Fenella, even if one ignored the earlier killing of Walter Brown, which had been to some extent excusable in view of the stevedore's own vicious conduct.

And always uppermost in his mind when he brooded on the subject of his arrest and trial was the thought of the revenge he would take on the man who had been most instrumental in catching him and the rest of the Roxy gang red-handed: none other than Detective Inspector Roy Denver. It was this anticipation of eventual and certain vengeance that was one of the few solaces in the long slow days and nights of his dreary incarceration. One day he would get Denver. One day he would kill the bastard.

Never for a moment did he entertain the notion that the arrest had been completely impersonal, that Denver had simply been carrying out his duty in spreading the net that had enmeshed the criminals and that he had done it with no feeling of vindictiveness towards Heeney or any of the others who had been caught with him. Heeney did not see the matter in this light because he did not wish to see it so; he needed an object on which or on whom to vent his spite and his bitterness and ultimately his vengeance; and that object was Roy Denver.

Heeney had served about a year of his sentence when he received news of an event which almost sent him into a frenzy of frustration. This event was the rehousing of Mrs Heeney in one of the high-rise blocks of flats that the Seaport authorities had caused to be erected to replace the old slum housing which was to be demolished.

When the news came through to him Mrs Heeney had already been installed for a couple of weeks in her new home; she was an infrequent letter-writer and had visited her son on only two occasions since the start of his imprisonment; the journey to Parkways was a long one and she said she could not afford the rail fare. When Heeney received the brief and scarcely legible letter which informed him of the move he realised that he had been too lax in allowing things to drift; he should have told his mother about the cash-box hidden under the floor of the privy and should have instructed her to dig it up and take it with her.

Now it was too late; she could not possibly go back to

the old place and start digging around, even if no work on the demolition and reconstruction had yet started there. He would not ask her to do it; she was a stupid old bitch and would be bound to make a mess of the job. Somebody might see her at it, might see her carrying the cash-box away; and the coppers might get on to her anyway, because she was bound to talk about it; he could not trust her not to go blabbing about his affairs when he was no longer around to keep her under control.

So maybe on the whole it was as well that he had never told her about the money, and perhaps it might lie undisturbed where it was for years yet. There was no telling when the terrace would be pulled down and he might be out of jail in time to go and pick up the cache himself. He had to hope so, but it nearly drove him crazy thinking about it, because there was a sum of ten thousand six hundred and fifty pounds in the black metal box and he would need that for starters when he came out.

The years he spent in Parkways seemed the longest and most wearisome of his life; the days and weeks and months passed at such a leaden pace that he sometimes had the feeling that all the clocks in the world had stopped, or that he had become trapped in a time capsule and would remain in it for ever. He hated prison life: the monotony, the boredom, the discomfort, the overcrowded cells, the sound of clanging doors and keys rattling in locks, the regimentation, the discipline, the very feel and smell of the place. He endured it all because he had to, and looked forward to the day when he would exact a price for all this wasted time, this great unproductive chunk carved out of his life. And the man who would pay that price was Denver; one day that swine of a copper would regret ever having put the bracelets on Douglas Heeney; you bet he would.

When the wicket at the entrance of the prison opened

and Heeney was practically thrust out once more into the wide world of freedom from which he had been untimely snatched he was greeted by a downpour of rain that was falling steadily from a grey and murky sky. It was the only welcome he had, for there was no one there to meet him. He was not disappointed, for he had expected no one. His mother was hardly likely to have made the journey, nor would he have wanted her to do so; and there was no one else who would have been sufficiently interested in his release even if they had known about it.

He travelled back to Seaport by train, and was on edge all the way, knowing that soon he would discover whether or not the money was still where he had left it. Having arrived at his destination he left the Haig Street Station and made his way immediately not to his mother's new home but to that street where he had been brought up.

It was apparent at once that the worst had happened: the terrace no longer existed; the entire area had been flattened in preparation for the rebuilding which had not yet started. Amid this desolation he could not tell even where the privy had been; there was not a clue to lead him to the spot where his treasure had been hidden; he could have hunted for a month, digging here, there and everywhere, and in the end not found it.

Even if it was still there!

And of that he could not be certain. Maybe a fortunate bulldozer driver had turned it up; maybe the cash had been shared out among a gang of happy demolition workers who had had a high old time on his money, not giving a damn.

Heeney stood there, gazing at this desert that was the wreck of his hopes and feeling the bitterness of his disappointment. Now he had nothing; he was back again to square one and had to make a fresh start from scratch. It was galling; he thought of what he could have done with that ten thousand pounds, and it was one more addition to the score that he had to settle with Detective Inspector Roy Denver.

And it would be settled; oh, it certainly would be settled in full; no doubt about that.

NINE

Old Pal

Heeney was amazed when he got his first sight of the block of flats in which his mother had come to roost. He had been looking for something all bright and new and sparkling, but what he saw was a structure that had already become dingy and depressing. He doubted whether there had ever been any real sparkle about it; yet it should not have deteriorated quite so quickly. But these concrete buildings had been doomed from the start: badly designed and poorly constructed, they had proved easy victims to the English climate and the English vandal.

It was probable that a woman as slatternly as Mrs Heeney would very quickly have made a pigsty of any new accommodation, however well designed and constructed it might have been; and with the material with which she had been provided she had had no trouble at all in converting it into a little haven of squalor. Looking round it, Heeney came to the conclusion that it would have been little better than the cell in Parkways if it had not been for the fact that he was free to leave it whenever he might feel the urge to do so.

The reunion between mother and son was muted; there were no raptures of delight on either side. Heeney gave the woman a peck on the cheek which had to pass for a filial kiss, and Mrs Heeney gave a little sniff which might have indicated that tears of joy were not far away but were being bravely held in check.

'You look thin, Duggie,' she said.

'I always was thin, Ma. You're looking okay.'

In fact she was looking much the same as she had been when he had left her; a little older, a little more slovenly perhaps. She was drawing the pension now and doing some part-time charring work to help with the expenses.

'It's nice to have you home again, son.'

He did not say it was nice to be home; he was still feeling too depressed by the loss of his nest-egg. The dreariness of this habitation to which he had returned did nothing to raise his spirits and banish the thought of that recent disappointment. But he could not blame her for that; she had never known about the money; he had never mentioned it to her.

She must have noticed how miserable he appeared to be when really he ought to have been over the moon as a free man for the first time in years.

'What's wrong, Duggie? You look down in the mouth. Why?'

'I've had a loss,' he said. There was no need to keep it from her now. Let her have a share of the disappointment.

'What loss?' she asked.

'Give's a fag and I'll tell you,' he said.

She searched around and found a packet. He took a cigarette and lighted it, sucking tobacco smoke into lungs that had been starved of this luxury for too long. 'I had a tin of money what I hid under the floor of our old privy.'

She looked concerned. 'You never!'

'I did. I been back there today and the houses are all gone. Everything's been knocked down and carted away. Now I've got sod all.'

'How much was there, Duggie?'

'Ten grand, and more.'

'Ten thousand pounds! You're having me on.'

'Why in hell would I be having you on? There'd be no point in it.'

'But wherever did you get ten thousand pounds?'

'Never mind where. What's the odds?' Heeney spoke savagely, taking out his frustration on the only person immediately available. 'I got it and now it's gone. Ten grand down the bloody drain.'

'Oh dear! All that money! You could've used something like that now you're out.'

'Of course I could've used it. That's what it was there for, wasn't it? It was to give me a fresh start. Now some bastard of a demolition hand has maybe got it. Or spent it. Taken the wife and kids on a luxury holiday to the Bahamas as like as not, whooping it up. On my money.'

Mrs Heeney sat down abruptly, as though all this had been just too much for her legs. 'You should've told me about it. I could've brought it here when they moved me. Why didn't you tell me?'

'I didn't know this was going to happen, did I?'

'You should've told me anyway.' Mrs Heeney sounded reproachful. 'Don't you trust your old mum?'

'Forget it,' Heeney said. 'It makes no difference now. I'll have to make my way without it; that's all.'

'Such a lot of money! I never dreamt you had so much. Dear, oh dear!'

'Well, don't go blabbing about it,' Heeney said. Already he had a feeling that it had been unwise to tell her. She was not to be trusted to keep it to herself; and though it might not bring any repercussions if other people heard the story there would be some sniggering behind his back if nothing worse. 'This is just between you and me, see?'

'Of course. You don't have to worry about that. Who would I tell it to?'

'I don't know. But don't; that's all.'

'All right, I won't. But all that lovely money! Gone! It's a shame, so it is. What'll you do now?'

Heeney drew hungrily on his cigarette. 'Do! I don't know. I'll have to think of something.'

'Couldn't you get a job?'

'Talk sense,' Heeney said. 'Who'd give me a job?'

'You could go and try the employment office.'

'Sod the employment office!' Heeney said. 'I'll manage without that bloody lot.'

The day after his release from prison he started moving around, picking up threads, getting the feel of this world that had moved on while he had been standing still. He succeeded in contacting Snappy Deacon, who had been given a shorter sentence than he had and had been out for more than a year. Deacon was living with a woman named Maggie Jones, who had been his girl-friend before he went inside. It appeared that she had visited him regularly during his imprisonment and had been waiting for him when he came out. She was obviously the faithful type, but she was no beauty and Heeney figured that she might have had difficulty in finding anyone to take Snappy's place.

Maggie Jones had a steady job in a biscuit factory and she rented a small basement flat in one of the less affluent districts near the river. Heeney knew the address because Deacon had taken him there a few times for a meal. Maggie was a good cook and she kept the flat in decent enough order.

It was afternoon when Heeney made his way there, and by good luck he found Deacon at home by himself. He had been watching the racing on television, but he switched it off and made Heeney welcome with every evidence of being delighted to see him.

'When did you get out?'

'Yesterday,' Heeney said.

'And none too soon neither, I'll bet. Well, sit yourself down and take the weight off your feet. Fancy a beer?'

'Thanks.'

Deacon fetched a couple of cans from the refrigerator and handed one to Heeney. 'Don't want a glass, do you?'

'No; this is fine.'

They drank beer and were silent for a while, looking at each other, remembering. Then Deacon said:

'How're you fixed? Moneywise.'

Heeney made a grimace. 'Next door to skint.'

'Is that a fact?' Deacon appeared surprised. 'I had you taped for one of the careful sort. I thought you'd have had your little pot of gold stashed away somewhere.'

'I had; but things went wrong.'

'Ah!' Deacon said. He did not ask what had gone wrong, and Heeney did not elaborate. 'So now you're on your uppers?'

'Just about.'

Deacon swallowed some beer. 'Reckon we'll have to think of something, won't we?'

'You got anything in mind?'

'Maybe,' Deacon said. 'But we'll talk about that later. Oh my, it seems a long time since we last had a talk, you and me.'

'It is a long time. Have you ever wondered how the coppers got on to us the way they did?'

'Bet your life I've wondered.'

'Any ideas?'

'My guess is one of us must've let something slip. There's no other way they could've got to know.'

'Well, it wasn't me,' Heeney said.

'I didn't think it was. And I know it wasn't me neither.'

'So that leaves three.'

'We can leave out Joe; he'd be as close as a clam. Which leaves either Billy Wadkins or Jerry Mouncer. I'd say one of them, or maybe both, had a bit too much to drink and let the old tongue wag in a public place. It happens. Nothing we can do about it now. Best to forget it. Just one of them things.'

Deacon was being philosophical, but Heeney was less inclined to forget.

'How would it have got to the ears of the law?'

'It's pretty certain that somebody must've picked up the message and handed it on.'

'Can you think of anyone who might have done the grassing job?'

'Well,' Deacon said, 'I did hear a whisper that Lugs Lacon used to do a bit of snouting for Denver when he was still in the force.'

'When he was still in the force! You mean to say he's out of it now?'

'Yes. Didn't you know?'

'It's news to me. I thought he'd be a bloody super by now.'

'Not him. I believe he's working for himself these days, but I haven't seen anything of him since that time he caught us at it. Anyway he's not a copper now, so we don't have to worry about him any more.'

'No,' Heeney said, with an enigmatic grin, 'we don't have to worry about him. Never again we don't.' And then he began to laugh.

'What's so funny?' Deacon asked. 'If there's a joke somewhere, why not share it with an old pal?'

Heeney stopped laughing as suddenly as he had begun. 'No joke,' he said. 'No joke at all. Especially for our Mr Denver.'

Deacon gave him a puzzled look. 'Sometimes, Duggie,' he said, 'I just don't get you. Sometimes I have this odd feeling that you live in a different world from the rest of us.'

'Maybe I do,' Heeney said. 'Maybe I do at that.'

He was still at the flat when Maggie Jones came home. It seemed to him that she had put on a bit of weight since he had last seen her, and she was still as plain as a gatepost. He wondered what Deacon saw in her.

'Hello, Mag,' he said. 'How're things with you?'

She appeared far less delighted to see him than Deacon had been; in fact she sounded distinctly cool. 'Oh,' she said, 'so you're out now.'

'Looks like it.'

She gave a sniff. 'Well, just mind they don't shove you back in again.'

'I'll try to do that,' Heeney said.

Deacon came to the door with him when he left and took the opportunity to slip a couple of ten-pound notes into his pocket.

'Just something to help you along till things get better. You can pay me back when they do. I'll be in touch.'

'Thanks, Snappy,' Heeney said. And then: 'I don't think Maggie likes me.'

'Take no notice,' Deacon said. 'Fact is she's got this bee in her bonnet about me going straight. Says I should get an honest job, else maybe I'll be back in stir. I guess she thinks with you around there'll be less chance of me listening to her advice.'

'What chance would there be if I wasn't around?'

Deacon gave a grin. 'None.'

Heeney nodded. 'That's about what I thought.'

Heeney found Denver's address in the phone book and went out that way to take a look at the house. There was no sign of the ex-detective anywhere around and the place looked deserted. But the house had an air of class about it, even though it was old and could have used a coat of paint. Denver seemed to be doing all right for himself now that he had left the police, and this fact gave an extra twist to Heeney's resentment.

He was still hanging around in the quiet tree-lined road when a woman drove up in a white Mini and turned in at the gateway. From the glimpse he had of her as she went past Heeney judged that she was quite young; she had reddish brown hair and was a real good-looker. She parked the Mini in front of the house and let herself in with a key, so it was evident that she was living there and was presumably either Denver's wife or his girl-friend. The bastard had everything going for him.

But the sight of Miss West, though it had added yet more fuel to the fire of Heeney's animosity, had set vague plans revolving in his mind. Maybe there would be a part for her to play in the scenario that was gradually taking shape. Give it time, just give it time.

It was two days later when chance brought his first encounter with Roy Denver himself since his commitment to prison. It happened in the afternoon rush hour when the traffic was snarled up not far from the entrance to Haig Street Station. As he was strolling along the pavement he suddenly caught sight of Denver sitting behind the wheel of one of the stationary cars.

In fact the blue Sierra was drawn up by the kerb no more than six feet away from him, and with scarcely a moment's pause for thought he stretched out an arm and grasped the handle on the nearside door. As luck would have it the door was not locked and he slipped into the seat beside the driver.

He could tell that Denver had not immediately recognised him, but the man's memory must have got to work pretty rapidly and he had the name on his tongue in a matter of seconds. It was because of his training no doubt; coppers were practised in the art of remembering faces and fitting names to them.

'Duggie Heeney!'

Oh yes, he remembered all right, and it might have made him just the least bit uneasy to find Heeney sitting there beside him. It must have been so totally unexpected.

Not that he showed any signs of uneasiness; he would have more control over himself than that. And there would be the question of pride; it would have been lowering to his self-esteem to have given any hint that Heeney's sudden appearance had given him the slightest cause for alarm.

But Heeney could sense the questions that were forming themselves in Denver's mind; and as they travelled along Haig Street and Exeter Street and up Calthorpe Hill he made it his business to give a little boost now and then to any suspicions Denver might have had regarding his intentions of getting his own back for all those miserable wasted years in Parkways Prison. And he knew that the swine was getting the message, getting it loud and clear, even though he had to be guarded in what he said, not making any direct threat in so many words but leaving it to be inferred.

So when they parted and Denver drove away in the blue Sierra he knew the man would not forget his existence; always now the thought of him would be at the back of Denver's mind, pestering, harassing, never giving him any rest, never permitting him the feeling of security that he might otherwise have enjoyed. Never.

And so at that parting, as he watched the car going away up the hill, Heeney gave his savage grin and spoke through clenched teeth, letting the venom spill out of him in a few bitter words of ill omen.

'So long, dead man!'

TEN
New Set-Up

Denver went to see Kenneth Roper at the Micro Plastics works with some reluctance. He had allowed Valerie to make the appointment with her employer because she seemed so keen to do so, but he was still far from enthusiastic about the arrangement and could see little good coming from it. He wondered whether she had put as much pressure on the Whizzkid to bring about the meeting as she had on him, and he thought it highly probable. Yet there was no hint in Roper's manner when they shook hands that he was not thoroughly pleased to see the security consultant.

'Good morning, Mr Denver. I'm glad you were able to come.'

Roper was in his private office, which was very modern in style without being in the least ostentatious. Valerie herself had ushered the visitor in, but had then retired from sight; which was something of a relief to Denver, since her presence might have been rather an embarrassment to him.

It was the first time he had come face to face with Kenneth Roper, though he had seen pictures of him in the local press from time to time. It could not be denied that he was a handsome man, though seen at close quarters he seemed a little older than he had in the photographs; perhaps the continual strain of being a go-getter tended to wear people more than the quiet life, and Roper had a few creases around the mouth and eyes and a sprinkling of grey in his hair that gave an impression of approaching middle age rather than enduring youth. But any satisfaction Denver might have derived from this fact was immediately cancelled out by the reflection that women were inclined to fall for just that touch of elegant maturity.

'I always try to keep a business appointment,' he said. 'It gives a bad impression not to.'

Roper smiled. 'Miss West tells me you're just the man to consult on matters of security.'

'She would, wouldn't she? She gives a very good account of you, too.'

This time Roper laughed. 'She does, does she? Well, that's nice to know.'

'I suppose you realise this was all her idea. I expect she coerced you into agreeing to it.'

'Oh,' Roper said, 'I wouldn't go as far as to say that. Not coerced.'

'You mean she just twisted your arm a bit?'

'Only in the nicest possible way.'

'Look,' Denver said; 'don't let me waste any more of your time. I'm sure you're a busy man. Just say you don't need my services and I'll leave. Then we'll both have done our duty. Right?'

Roper shook his head. 'Oh, no; it wouldn't look right. Anyway, I've got some time put aside for this business, so how about you and me taking a tour round the place? You may find it interesting.'

'I'm sure I will. If you really don't mind.'

'Let's go then,' Roper said.

It was certainly interesting, and Roper did his best to explain in simple terms just what was going on; but a lot of it was far too technical for Denver to understand. He had never had more than the haziest of ideas regarding the way in which microchips and printed circuits and computers worked, and it was hardly likely that a fifty-minute crash course on the subject would leave him much more enlightened. He did, however, get an impression of a thriving high-technology enterprise going flat out to create products that would have a world market. In the context of unemployment and the demise of the old heavy industries it was an encouraging augury for the future.

The Micro Plastics plant had little of the appearance of an old-style factory. The plain single-storey concrete buildings with their corrugated asbestos roofs were well spaced out, and there were flower beds and shrubs and young trees growing here and there, which gave the whole site a pleasantly landscaped aspect. Completely surrounding it was a high chain-link fence supported on concrete posts, and at the main entrance was a gatehouse and a yellow-and-white striped bar which lifted to let traffic through.

Denver made one or two suggestions of a fairly general nature regarding security, but he knew it was merely going through the motions and he guessed that Roper knew it too. Security was probably as tight as a drum already, and no doubt the biggest threat that Micro Plastics faced was industrial espionage.

After nearly an hour they seemed to come to a tacit agreement to call the charade off. Roper accompanied Denver back to where he had left the Sierra.

'It's been pleasant meeting you, Roy,' he said. During the tour of inspection they had got themselves on to first name terms. 'Sure you wouldn't like a drink?'

'Thanks, but no. I never take any when I have to drive.'

'Very wise. It's a pity there aren't more like you. There'd be fewer killed on the roads.'

It had been a very cordial tour, and rather against his inclination Denver had found himself quite taking to the Whizzkid; there was really nothing about him you could actively dislike. This fact, however, made him no easier in his mind when he thought of Valerie as the industrialist's confidential secretary. And Roper not married. Which was a pity.

It was almost as though the man had been reading his thoughts, for he remarked suddenly, for no apparent reason: 'Valerie is a splendid girl. The best secretary I've ever had. I'd hate to lose her.'

'So would I,' Denver said. And he hoped Roper had not meant it in quite the same way.

'You're a lucky man, Roy. But you don't need me to tell you that. You know it well enough already.'

'Yes, I do know it. The only snag is, I can't be certain just how long the luck will last.'

'Ah,' Roper said, 'that's something none of us can be sure about, isn't it?'

'I suppose so.'

'You won't forget to send me your account, will you?'

'There won't be one,' Denver said. 'What have I done to earn a fee?'

'You've given me some of your time.'

'And you've given me some of yours, which is probably worth a great deal more.'

'Well,' Roper said, 'it's up to you.'

He arrived home before Valerie. When she came in the first thing she asked was:

'Well? How did it go?'

'Hasn't the Whizzkid told you?'

'No, he hasn't. And please, Roy, I do wish you'd stop calling him that. It's a bit childish, isn't it?'

'Maybe you're right.'

'Did you like him?'

'Oddly enough, I did.'

'I don't see that there's anything odd about it. He's a likeable man, isn't he?'

'Yes, he is,' Denver said; and he almost added: 'Damn him!' But he restrained himself because he doubted whether it would have gone down very well with Miss West, even if he explained the reason for the addition. She might have gone up in the air if he had admitted that he was not a little jealous of Kenneth Roper, since it might imply that he did not fully trust her in the likeable man's company.

'So,' she asked again, 'how did it go?'

'On the security front it didn't.'

She frowned. 'How do you mean?'

'I mean he's got all the security he needs. He doesn't require my services as a consultant.'

She was obviously disappointed. 'I don't think you could really have tried to sell yourself to him.'

'Well, I certainly didn't go down on my hands and knees and beg for the job, if that's what you mean.'

'Don't be an idiot.' She sounded a trifle snappish. 'Well, I suppose it was only to be expected. You didn't have your heart in it right from the start. I ought to have known better than to try and help you to drum up some custom.'

'No,' Denver said, 'don't think that. It was very sweet of you, and please don't imagine I'm not grateful. But it just wouldn't have worked out. He knew it and I knew it. Apart from that we got on fine.'

'Apart, you mean, from the sole purpose of the meeting. Ah well; I suppose I should be thankful that you acted in a civilised manner.'

'Don't I always?' Denver said.

In another part of the town another conference was taking place. There were three people taking part, and if he had seen them Duggie Heeney might have recognised them as the three skinheads he had recently encountered on his way back to his mother's flat. One of them had a bandage on his right wrist; it had not in fact been broken by Heeney's blow with the iron rod, but it had been cut and bruised and was still painful. This man's name was Rod Joby, and he had a pale complexion and slightly hooded eyes which gave him a sleepy look.

One of the others had a mark on his throat, which was also the result of Heeney's work; it was a scab that would develop into a scar and probably be there for the duration of his life. His name was Sid Hunt and he was all skin and bone, gaunt of face, as though he were suffering from some wasting disease.

The third one, Dave Mellor, was fat and pimply. He was the one who had been using the knuckleduster, and he had a stiff neck and sore ribs. All three of them had good reason to remember the meeting with Duggie Heeney, and they were stirred to anger by the memory.

'He's an ex-con,' Joby said. 'He was done for a warehouse job and resisting arrest. He ain't bin out long.'

'Howja know?' Hunt asked.

'I bin making inquiries, haven't I? How else would I know? He's got a bit of a reputation as a hard case.'

'Sounds like bad news to me,' Mellor said uneasily. He was the least courageous of the three, easily led but nervous. 'Maybe we should leave him alone.'

'Never,' Joby said. 'No way. Not after what he done to us. What you say, Sid?'

'I'm with you, Rod,' Hunt said. 'You can count on me. All the way.'

The conference was taking place in an old motor-van that had been stripped of everything useable and illegally dumped on some waste ground. The three young men used it as a kind of low-grade clubhouse where they drank cheap red wine, smoked cannabis and snorted cocaine when they could afford it. They had started as kids by sniffing glue and had gone on from there as they grew older, graduating to the harder stuff.

Sometimes they chased the dragon with heroin, and they had tried the amphetamines for kicks. None of them had ever had a steady job and they had given up all expectation of having one.

'We'll get our own back,' Joby said. 'We'll do that bastard if it takes for ever.'

'Yes, but how?' Mellor asked. 'he's clever. He'll be on the look-out and he knows how to take care of hisself. See what he done to us.'

'There's three of us,' Joby said. 'He was lucky that time cause we wasn't expecting it. Next time it'll be different. there'll be a way. We got the time.'

Heeney himself had scarcely given a thought to the skinheads since the evening when he had dealt with them so severely. Even the warning shouted after him as he walked away had not made him at all uneasy; punks like that were just not worth his consideration. And he had more important things to think about.

But Joby had found out where Heeney lived, and sometimes he kept watch and noted when Heeney left the building, taking care that he himself should not be seen by the man who was the object of his interest.

Joby told the others: 'He lives with his old mum in a flat on the sixth floor. I been there.'

'Why don't we bust in while he's at home?' Hunt suggested. 'Take him by surprise and give him the works.'

But Joby was not in favour of this. 'It's too risky. And the old woman would be there. She'd be screaming bloody murder.'

'So what do we do then?'

'I'll think of something,' Joby said.

But Heeney was not listening and he was not worrying either. He still had other business on his mind and the skinheads had no part in it.

*

'Have you seen anything more of that man?' Valerie asked.

Denver looked at her questioningly. 'What man?'

'You know. The one who's just out of prison. The one who threatened you.'

'Oh, you mean Duggie Heeney. No, I haven't seen him again. I doubt whether I shall.'

'You don't think he'll do anything?'

'No,' Denver said. 'He's like a lot of these ex-cons; when they're inside they make fine plans to take revenge on the men who sent them there; sometimes it's the police, sometimes the judge; but when they come out it all fades away in words. Heeney's no different from all the others; he won't do anything.'

But he knew that he was not telling her the truth. Heeney was different from the others; there was a streak of venom in him that set him apart. That was why he would bear watching, why it would be advisable to stay on the alert. The snag was that you could never stay alert all the time; there were bound to be occasions when you let your guard down; and then you became vulnerable.

He wondered whether Heeney had a plan. Perhaps. He was probably a crafty little villain; not terribly brainy maybe but well endowed with low cunning. He was also a man with none of the scruples that tended to put a rein on the actions of a normal person. In a word he was dangerous. Or in a shorter word: deadly.

Denver had assured Miss West that he was not worried about Heeney, but this again was not altogether true. There were little doubts in his mind, and every time he thought of Heeney he could not help wondering just what the man was doing and what he intended to do. But he would never have admitted as much.

'Don't worry,' he said. 'There's no reason why you should be at all concerned about that nasty piece of work.'

And oddly enough, though he did not know it, for the present this was in fact so. For Heeney had more immediate and urgent business to attend to. Having lost the ten thousand pounds that had been hidden in the old privy, he had no soft cushion of money to rest on while he made a leisurely assessment of the prospects open to him. So before he could allow himself the luxury of dealing with the former Detective Inspector Roy Denver he had to make some cash, and for him the one thing this did not mean was getting an honest job. Meanwhile, Denver would have to wait. Let him sweat for a time; it would do no harm; he was not likely to run away.

Heeney had another meeting with Snappy Deacon at the Boundary Greyhound Stadium. It was where they had had their first encounter and it was as good a place as any for a heart-to-heart talk. It was better than the flat, where Maggie might walk in on them, because there were matters it would have been inadvisable to discuss in her presence.

'Mag's all right,' Deacon said, 'but she's too honest. It's her only fault. Still, you can't have everything.'

They made a few bets on the dogs before getting down to the real business of the evening. Heeney had a couple of small wins and Deacon gave him a slap on the back.

'Must be your lucky night.'

Heeney was using the money Deacon had given him, but there was not much of it left. He hoped Snappy had some good news for him, because things were getting a bit tight and nothing had turned up. He had even been tempted to try the old game of burglary, but this would have meant having dealings with Alfred Waite and he was reluctant to go back to that old skinflint. Still, something had to be done; a man could not live on air.

It was later when Deacon came out with the

information which so far he had been keeping to himself.

'I've fixed it,' he said. 'He's agreed to see you.'

'When?'

'Tomorrow evening. We have to be at his place at nine o'clock. That okay with you?'

Heeney said it was.

'You'll find him a bit different from Joe Roxy.'

'May be just as well. I was never all that keen on our Joe.'

'He had his faults, I won't deny. But we've finished with him now.'

'Seen anything of him lately?'

'No. He seems to have disappeared since he came out. Maybe he's trying his luck down south. Same with Billy and Jerry. Them days is over; it's a complete new set-up this time; new guv'nor, new way of running things. You'll see.'

'You think I'll fit in?'

'Sure you will. Just treat him with respect and he'll take you on. I've recommended you to him, so you only have to play your cards right and it's a pushover.'

'I hope so,' Heeney said. 'I need some scratch.'

'Don't we all?' Deacon said.

ELEVEN

Mr G

The house was on Highman's Avenue, out in that same
classy residential district where years ago as a youth
Heeney had been taken by Humphrey in his Jaguar.
The memory of that episode came into Heeney's mind,
but it meant nothing to him now; it had just been a small
piece of his education, long past and done with; and he
had never seen the man again. For all he knew
Humphrey might be dead; and good riddance to bad
rubbish if he was.

This time he travelled in Snappy Deacon's car, a not
very new Vauxhall which was commonplace enough to
be quite inconspicuous. Heeney himself had once
thought about buying a car, and he had taken a course
of driving lessons but had never applied for a test and
had no licence. But he reckoned he could still drive a car
if the need should ever arise.

'You'll just call him Mr G,' Deacon said. 'We all do.'

'How do you spell that? G and two e's?'

'No; it's just the letter. Like an initial, see.'

'Doesn't he have a name?'

'I suppose so, but I don't know what it is and I've
never asked. If he likes to be called Mr G I'm not
arguing. And you'd better not, neither.'

'It don't bother me,' Heeney said. 'He could call

himself the King of Siam and it'd be all one far's I'm concerned.'

Deacon parked the Vauxhall in a quiet spot and they walked the last part of the way.

'Why don't we drive right up to the house?' Heeney asked.

'Because we don't, that's why.' Deacon sounded a trifle irritated. 'Look, Duggie, if you don't like doing things his way you better call it off right here and now. Is that what you want?'

Heeney was quick to placate him. 'No, no. I was only asking. I'm willing to follow the routine. Don't be so touchy.'

'All right then. Let's go.'

They came to a high wall with a door in it. The door was locked but Deacon had a key. He opened the door and when they were both on the other side of the wall he locked it again. No one had been anywhere around to see them.

As far as Heeney could make out they were in a private garden, though it was too dark to see anything clearly. But Deacon obviously knew the way and Heeney just followed close behind him. There was soft turf underfoot and trees and shrubs loomed up here and there as they progressed. They went through an archway in another wall and the house appeared in front of them. They crossed a paved area that was probably a kind of courtyard and came to the back door. Deacon rang a bell and the door was opened with very little delay by a bald-headed man with a bruiser's face who was wearing black trousers and a butler's waistcoat. In spite of the garb he looked more like a nightclub bouncer than a manservant, and his voice was so hoarse it seemed the words had difficulty in getting out of his throat.

'So it's you, Mr Deacon. And that'll be Mr Heeney with you, no doubt.'

'Yes,' Deacon said, 'this is Mr Heeney. You're sounding a bit wheezy, Marcus.'

'It's me tubes, Mr Deacon. They ain't what they used to be, not by a long chalk.'

'What is? Mr G's at home, is he?'

'Where else would he be? He's expecting you. You better come inside.'

They went in. There was a big kitchen on the right, and Marcus led the way up three steps to a short passageway and a door on the left which opened into a room with the appearance of a library. Shelves round the walls were filled with books and there was an open fireplace with a black iron grate stacked with unlit logs. Heavy velvet curtains were drawn across the windows and there were chairs upholstered in dark red leather. A long narrow table made of oak that was almost as dark as the ironwork stood in the middle of the room, but there was nothing on it.

'You're to wait here,' Marcus said. He went away, closing the door behind him.

'Nice lot of books,' Deacon said.

Heeney sniffed. 'Books! Who reads 'em?'

'Maybe Mr G does.'

A lot of the books looked old, many of them bound in tooled calfskin; they could have been collector's items, rare and valuable. But Heeney had no taste in that line and he dismissed them with a contemptuous glance.

They had been waiting for about five minutes when the door was again opened by Marcus and a man in an electric wheel-chair came into the room. He steered the chair round to the fireplace side of the oak table and brought it to a stop facing the door.

'That will be all, Marcus,' he said. 'You may go.'

Marcus left the room and closed the door.

Heeney was staring at the occupant of the wheel-chair, who was a heavily-built man, rather handsome, wearing gold-rimmed glasses and possessing a mass of silvery hair which spilled down over his ears and collar. He was neatly dressed in a dark grey pin-stripe suit and black shoes polished to a glossy brilliance.

The man met Heeney's stare and responded to it with a faint smile. 'I am Mr G,' he said. His voice was cultured, softly modulated, under perfect control; it seemed to have a caressing quality. But the eyes behind the glasses were hard and coldly calculating; they did not match the voice.

Heeney glanced at Deacon. 'You didn't tell me.' It sounded like an accusation of bad faith.

It was Mr G who replied. 'He did not tell you I was a chair-bound cripple? That is because I instructed him not to. A small surprise for you, Mr Heeney. Life is full of surprises, wouldn't you say?'

Heeney had a feeling that Mr G was making game of him, and he resented it. It was evident that the man considered himself mentally superior, and he could have been right. Perhaps he really did read those books. Yet when you got down to the basics he was still a crook.

'Deacon tells me you're looking for employment. Of a kind.'

'I'm available,' Heeney said, a trifle grumpily. 'If the job is right.'

'Of course you are. And I have Deacon's word for it that you're a reliable man.'

'He's that all right, Mr G,' Deacon put in. 'I've worked with him and I know. We can use someone like him.'

'Possibly so. How are you with guns, Heeney?'

Heeney noticed that Mr G had already dropped the 'Mr' when addressing him.

'How d'you mean?' he asked.

'I mean can you handle a pistol or perhaps a pump-action shotgun?'

'Reckon I could if the shooters was there to use.'

'But you haven't had the experience?'

'Well, no, not as such. But there's nothing to it, is

there? You point the gun and pull the trigger and that's it. Bang, bang, you're dead.'

'If you're stupid enough to believe that,' Mr G said icily, 'I may have to think again about taking you on. The kind of man I need should have at least a smattering of brains.'

Heeney was stung and he flushed angrily. 'Now look, mister –'

'No!' Mr G's voice had hardened; it was incisive, no longer smooth and caressing. 'No, Heeney, you look. We're not playing kids' games. If you're going to work for me you'll have instruction in the proper use of firearms and I shall expect you to acquire the requisite skill. Is that understood?'

Heeney got his temper under control. There was no sense in getting heated just because this smoothie in the wheel-chair thought he was God Almighty.

'Sure. Anything you say, Mr G.'

Riding back in the Vauxhall Heeney came in for some criticism from Deacon.

'For a moment there,' Deacon said, 'I thought you'd blown it. Mr G doesn't like people to answer back.'

'To hell with Mr G. Guys like that with their fancy talk and their superior manners get on my wick. Who does he think he is?'

'He knows who he is. He's the boss, and you better remember it. You want the work, don't you?'

'I reckon so,' Heeney answered sulkily.

'Then you'll have to behave yourself. Obey orders and don't argue; that's the drill.'

Heeney was silent for a while. Then he said: 'Can't he use his legs at all.'

'Not much, I'd say. Me, I've never seen him out of the chair.'

'How'd he get to be that way?'

'I don't know. Polio, maybe. What's it matter? He's got

the brains and that's what counts.'

'Is Marcus the only one he has working in the house?'

'No; there's Marcus's wife as well. She's sort of cook-housekeeper. Then there's a man who does the garden and acts as chauffeur when needed.'

'Do they all know what goes on?'

'Don't ask me,' Deacon said. 'How would I know? It's none of my business. I just do as I'm told and take the money.'

'Ah yes,' Heeney said. 'The money.'

He received instruction in the use of a pistol from Marcus. He supposed Marcus would have been described as a butler, but it was apparent that he had other skills. The instruction took place in a basement underneath Mr G's house, which had been converted into a small shooting-range and armoury. Heeney proved to be an apt pupil and was eager to learn, so progress was rapid. After a very few lessons Marcus said he was satisfied.

'You'll do. We're not out to make a Bisley marksman of you. If you have to use a gun it'll likely be at short range. Okay?'

'Okay,' Heeney said. He had enjoyed the shooting lessons. He liked the feel of a gun in his hand; it gave him a sense of power. You could use a brick to kill a man, or even your bare hands, but a gun was something else again; like that woman long ago who had told him her name was Fenella, it had class.

He had seen nothing more of Mr G since the initial interview. Deacon told him that this was normal; Mr G was not in the habit of fraternising with the criminals in his organisation; he kept himself aloof and only spoke to them on matters of business, invariably addressing them by their surnames only. It was all rather feudal, and Heeney was still not completely happy with the system; but for the present he had decided to go along with it and see how things panned out.

About a week later he was summoned to a conference at Mr G's house. Deacon took him there in the Vauxhall.

'Something's moving,' Deacon said. 'This is the way it always starts. He'll have got it all planned out and he'll tell us what we have to do.'

'So we don't get a say in the planning?'

'No. We can make suggestions, of course; but he usually has everything right, so it's only a matter of asking a few questions if we aren't clear about anything.'

'Will anybody else be there?'

'I expect so; unless it's a very small job. And Mr G don't really go in for small jobs. This is where we get to see who we're working with.'

'Well, that'll be interesting if nothing else,' Heeney said. He had never met any other members of the gang. It seemed an odd way of going to work, but there was a lot that was odd about Mr G's set-up. Still, if it was successful, why quibble?

There were just two of them, and they were already there when he and Deacon arrived. Their names were Boyce and Landis, and they did not look like villains. Deacon knew them and introduced Heeney. They nodded but made no move to shake hands. The impression he got was one of anonymity; everything about them was average – height, build, weight. They were neither handsome nor ugly, but somewhere between the two, and they both had limp mousy hair that might have been clipped about two weeks ago. The suits they were wearing looked well-tailored without being flashy; they were not new but were not yet ready for the jumble sale.

'Anybody else coming?' Deacon asked.

'Don't think so,' Boyce said. 'Could be wrong, but I'd say not.'

Then Marcus pushed the door open and Mr G came

in with a whir of the electric motor. Marcus went away.

Mr G gave a nod to the four men gathered in the library. 'Good evening, gentlemen.' He steered the wheel-chair round the end of the table and halted it in front of the fireplace. He had a large-scale ordnance survey map resting on his knees and he spread it out on the table. There were markings on the map made in pencil, and there were also some sheets of paper with diagrams and figures on them.

'Now gather round and listen carefully,' he said.

TWELVE
According to Plan

It was cold and damp under the trees; there had been a heavy shower earlier in the evening and drops were still falling from the leaves now and then. Underfoot the ground was soft and spongy, and Heeney's feet were cold.

Just beyond the edge of the trees he could see the narrow ribbon of the private road which meandered for about half a mile before reaching the big country house to which it led. There was just enough moonlight penetrating the cloud cover to make it visible, but in the small wood where Heeney was standing it was almost completely dark, and he could sense rather than see Deacon waiting nearby on his right. Boyce was a few yards away on the left, while Landis was posted a quarter of a mile or so down the road where it joined the public highway to keep a sharp look-out and be ready to warn Boyce over the walkie-talkie radio as soon as he spotted the car they were waiting for.

The vehicle in which they had travelled the last part of the twenty-mile journey from Seaport, and which had been stolen and fitted with false number plates a couple of days earlier, was concealed a short distance from the junction. They had left it there and had proceeded on foot to their present position, carrying the three white traffic cones with them.

Heeney caught Deacon's whisper: 'It's a grand life if you don't weaken.'

Heeney just grunted; he was not amused. He wondered whether this was all going to turn out to be a waste of time, a right bloody fiasco. Mr G had had it all planned out, but had Mr G got his facts right? Would the car be there at the stated time, more or less, and would it be carrying what it was supposed to? These were big questions, and Heeney was not at all convinced that the answer to them was necessarily in the affirmative. For his part he had doubts. He could feel the hard metal of the Walther pistol in the pocket of his zipped-up leather jacket and he was fully prepared to use it; but would he get the chance?

Marcus had handed out the guns and had been at pains to impress on Heeney the fact that he was not to keep the pistol for his own private use but was to return it to the armoury when the job had been completed. Heeney had promised to bring it back and he supposed he had better do so, much as he would have liked to keep the weapon.

Suddenly there came a warning from Boyce. He had got the word from Landis that the car had turned off the highway and was heading towards them.

'Let's go.'

Heeney picked up the cone that was close beside him and carried it on to the narrow road. Boyce and Deacon each had a cone also, and they made a barrier across the road before quickly darting back into cover. A few moments later they saw the light from the headlamps of the approaching car.

Heeney wondered whether the driver would stop when he spotted the cones or whether he would suspect a trap and drive straight on, knocking them aside. If he did they would have to try to stop the car by shooting at it; but the operation would likely end in a cock-up if it came to that.

So it had better not.

The car was approaching at a moderate pace; the road surface was bad and it had never been made for speeding. The beam of the headlamps swept round a slight bend and picked up the white cones. Now was the moment when the driver might take alarm and step on the accelerator, going hard at the flimsy barrier; the trees on each side grew too closely to the road for him to take to the verge.

Heeney was holding his breath, waiting; but then he breathed freely again as the car slowed and came to a halt just a few yards from the line of cones.

Heeney had the Walther in his hand and was ready to go, but he had to wait for the signal from Boyce, and Boyce had not yet made it. In the car no one seemed to be moving, but by the reflected light of the headlamps it was possible to see that there were two men in the front and no one in the back.

The seconds passed, and still no one had made a move. It was obvious that the men in the car were suspicious and were not going to do anything precipitately; they probably had the doors locked and felt safer inside.

'Why don't we go and get them now?' Heeney demanded in a hissing whisper. He was eager to get it over and done with.

'No!' Boyce said. 'Wait!'

To Heeney it seemed crazy. The driver might decide to get the car moving again and they might lose the best chance they would have. He was fuming inwardly, but he was the new boy and he had to obey orders.

And Boyce was right. The door on the driver's side began to open slowly. A man's foot came cautiously out, then an arm and a head. The man's hand was holding something and it looked like a revolver.

'Now!' Boyce said.

He was in the lead and he was the one who got the

bullet in him. He gave a cry and fell away to the right. Heeney was close behind him and he shot the driver through the head. The man in the passenger seat also had a handgun, but he panicked and fired it wildly, so that the bullet went through the roof. He got no second chance; Heeney shot him, too, pumping three bullets into his chest in quick succession.

It had all happened in a matter of seconds and there were two dead men slumped on the front seats of the car. It was a new way of killing for Heeney and he loved it; it was so quick, so easy, so final.

He heard Boyce cursing and knew that he had not been killed by the driver's bullet. Boyce was on his feet and was holding his right arm with his left hand.

'You all right?' Deacon asked.

'No, I'm bloody well not all right,' Boyce snapped. 'Get the bags and let's get the hell out.'

There was good reason for haste; the shooting might have been heard in the house and somebody might come out to investigate. The sooner they were gone from there the better it would be.

Deacon reached inside the car to get the keys and went to the back to unlock the boot. There were two black suitcases inside, and Deacon and Heeney took one each. Then all three of them began to run back along the road. Boyce was still cursing but he seemed to be able to use his legs to good effect and he had picked up the dropped pistol before starting on his way. They were all wearing gloves to ensure that no fingerprints would be left to incriminate them.

Heeney was thankful there was not far to run, because the suitcase was damned heavy and he had a pain in the side when he reached the place where Landis was waiting with the stolen car. They loaded the suitcases into the boot and piled in. Landis was at the wheel and Heeney got in beside him leaving the rear seat for Deacon and the injured Boyce.

'So you had some trouble,' Landis said as he got the car moving. 'How bad is it?'

'Bad enough,' Boyce said, 'but I reckon I'll live.'

Heeney glanced over his shoulder and saw that Deacon was helping Boyce out of his jacket so that he could get at the wound. It was in the forearm and there was plenty of blood, but Boyce appeared to be able to move the arm without trouble, which indicated that no bones were broken. Deacon made a bandage with a couple of handkerchiefs to stanch the bleeding, and Heeney figured that with luck the bullet had just gouged its way through the flesh without doing too much damage. Nobody was talking about doctors or hospitals and he hoped there would be no need for surgery.

About halfway back to Seaport in a secluded spot they transferred themselves and the luggage to the Mercedes in which they had started the journey and discarded the stolen car. It had served its purpose and was no longer needed.

There was no one around when they opened the door in the wall at the rear of Mr G's house and carried the suitcases inside. Marcus let them into the house, and he looked at Boyce's arm and gave a shake of the head.

'Nasty.'

'It could've been a sight nastier,' Deacon said. 'He could've been killed.'

Mr G was waiting for them in the library. Deacon and Heeney put the suitcases on the table. Mr G scarcely glanced at them; he was looking at Boyce, whose right arm was in a mess.

'So you got yourself hurt.'

'A bit. They had guns.' Boyce's cheeks were pale and he looked sick.

Mr G nodded. 'It was to be expected. You had better go with Marcus and let him have a look at that arm. No need for you to wait here.'

Marcus was hovering in the doorway. Boyce went
away with him and Landis closed the door.

'A pity about that,' Mr G said. 'But these things will
happen. Otherwise everything went according to plan, I
imagine?'

'Yes,' Deacon said.

'And the other men. How many were there?'

'Two. They're dead.'

'Ah!'

'Heeney shot them,' Landis said.

Mr G looked at Heeney. 'So you used the gun.'

'Yes,' Heeney said.

'And enjoyed doing so, perhaps?'

'Somebody had to do it. It was the job,' Heeney said.
But he was thinking that Mr G was shrewd; it was as if
he could peer into your mind and read what was going
on in there.

'Yes, it was the job.' Mr G glanced again at the
suitcases, but he made no move to open them; it was
probable that they were locked. 'Now let me have an
account of all that happened.'

It was like a military debriefing, Heeney thought.
They had to tell him everything, leaving nothing out,
even the smallest detail. Now and then he broke in with
a question, but for the most part he was content to sit
and listen.

Finally there were a few brief words of congratulation
for the way in which they had carried out the
assignment, and then the handing out of the large
manila envelopes that had been waiting for them.
Heeney could feel that the envelope handed to him was
well filled; it was not the kind you could put in a pocket
without folding, but he did not open it and the other
two did not open theirs either.

When they left the library the two suitcases were still
unopened on the table. Heeney would have liked to see
what was inside, but he decided it was best not to

demand a view of the haul. He had to go by the book –
Mr G's book – like it or not.

Deacon took him home in the Vauxhall. They had
handed in their weapons before leaving, and Heeney
had done so with reluctance; he would greatly have
loved to keep the pistol, but that would have been
contrary to regulations. Mr G had no intention of
supplying any of his men with firearms for their
personal use.

'Well?' Deacon said. 'Are you satisfied?'

Heeney had torn open the manila envelope and had
found a total of ten thousand pounds inside in used
notes.

'It's nice money,' he said, 'but what I'd like to know is
what he's getting. How much was there in them two
suitcases?'

'I don't know.'

'Well, look at it this way. It was to have been payment
for a shipment of heroin them two guys was going to
pick up at the big house. Right?'

'That's what we was told, yes.'

'So my guess is there was a hell of a lot of money
involved, else why two cases? Maybe a million. Now ten
grand's not much compared to that. And what's our
bloody Mr G done for his whack?'

'He set it up, didn't he? Would you have known that
car was going to come along at that particular place at
that particular time? Would I have known? Would
Boyce or Landis? Not likely. So the way I look at it is
this: if Mr G can arrange these things so we each get a
nice little packet, it's okay by me.'

'Well, maybe,' Heeney said; but he was still thinking
of the possible million pounds in the suitcases and
reflecting that Mr G was being very well paid for his
part in the business. 'How do you reckon he got to
know?'

'The word is that he runs some kind of intelligence

network and gets supplied with the information that way. He has his spies, see. And I reckon it costs him a packet, so he needs plenty of the old spending money to finance it. You can't run that sort of organisation on the cheap.'

'So we're just little cogs in a big machine?'

'That's about it.'

Heeney was not so keen on being a little cog, however big and successful the machine might be; he had always had a liking for independence, a desire to be his own master. Even in the Roxy gang he had been irked by the touch of discipline that Joe Roxy imposed; but that had been nothing compared with Mr G's autocratic régime. With Joe you did know pretty well what was going on; you were in on the planning and you had a say in it; but with this lot you were practically in the dark, and if you raised your voice in argument you were quickly slapped down and told where you got off.

Still, ten grand was ten grand, and it almost made up what he had lost under the floor of the old privy. It also gave him a breathing-space, since he had been given to understand that there would be no more jobs for Mr G for a while and that he would be called when he was wanted again.

So now he could concentrate on that other business which had been left to simmer for a time. Now Mr Roy Denver could be brought back into focus and something could really be done about him.

THIRTEEN
The Big Fish

Heeney came up behind Lacon as he was walking along the pavement in Blythe Street. He took Lacon by the elbow and when this seedy individual gave a sidelong glance to see who had accosted him he seemed nervous.

'You're just the man I been looking for,' Heeney said. 'You and me, Lugs, we gotta have a little talk.'

Two days had passed since the snatching of the two suitcases of money, and still there had been nothing in the press or on TV concerning the discovery of two dead men in a car; so it looked as though the people from the big house had been first on the scene and had decided it was in their best interest to hush things up. If they were dealing in heroin in a big way the last thing they would want would be a police investigation taking place right under their noses. So maybe they had buried the bodies somewhere on the estate and had got rid of the bloodstained vehicle.

It suited Heeney, because it meant that he had nothing to worry about as far as the law was concerned. Not that he would have been in any danger of arrest anyway, since there would have been nothing to link him to the killings; but this made him even more secure and was all to the good. With the ten thousand pounds safely stowed away he was feeling rather pleased with life, and now Lugs Lacon had practically walked into his hands. It was obvious that luck was smiling on him.

'Why, Mr Heeney,' Lacon said; and he gave a sickly kind of grin. 'Fancy meeting you.'

Lacon was a rather sick-looking creature altogether. He was small and thin, with coat-hanger shoulders and a scraggy neck, and when he grinned wide gaps were revealed in his teeth. The skin of his face was like ancient writing-paper, yellowy and spotted, and the hair showing under the filthy old cloth cap he was wearing seemed dry and lifeless. His most prominent features were his ears, which had given rise to his nickname; they were so large as to be out of all proportion to his head, and they stood out almost at right angles, as if to catch the slightest whisper that might have been wafted in his direction.

He had tried a number of criminal activities in his time, never with any great success, and he had served various terms of imprisonment as a way of paying the debts he owed to society. Now he picked up a living as best he could; and judging by appearances it would have seemed that his best was not really good enough.

'Now,' Heeney said, 'why don't you and me go and have a pint somewhere and do a little in the heart-to-heart line. How does that strike you?'

Lacon's expression could hardly have been described as one of unalloyed delight at this suggestion, and he made a half-hearted attempt to free his arm, but Heeney kept a grip on it.

'I'd like to, Mr Heeney, straight I would; but I just don't have the time right now.'

Heeney echoed his words in undisguised disbelief. 'You don't have the time! Why, what do you have to do that's so bloody important it comes in the way of a nice cosy little chat over a jar with an old pal?'

Heeney was not an old pal of Lacon's and they both knew it, but Lacon made no attempt to deny the relationship. All he said was: 'I gotta see this man.'

'What man?'

'You wouldn't know him.'

'And what do you have to see him about that can't wait a little while?'

'Well, it's like this here; he may have a job for me, you see.'

'What kind of a job? Grassing?'

Lacon tried to give the impression of a man deeply wronged and deeply shocked. 'Whatever give you that idea? Would I do anything like that? I ask you. Be fair.'

For answer Heeney tightened his grip on Lacon's arm. 'Let's go and have that drink. I insist.'

'Well,' Lacon said, with every appearance of extreme reluctance, 'I s'pose I could spare a few minutes.'

There was a public-house no more than a short walk away and Heeney ushered Lacon into it. Seated at a table in a corner of the bar with two mugs of beer in front of them which Heeney had bought, they got down to the matter of the heart-to-heart talk. Not that Lacon, even with a swallow or two of the amber liquid inside him showed any inclination to become at all talkative; he just eyed Heeney across the table with an expression of extreme wariness and not a little apprehension.

'I hear you've been a naughty boy, Lugs,' Heeney said. 'A very naughty boy.'

'Howja mean?' Lacon asked.

'I think you know damn well what I mean. It was you as got me, along with three colleagues of mine, put under lock and key for a period of years.'

'Me!' Lacon's eyebrows shot up so high they almost vanished under the peak of the cap.

'Yes, you, Lugs, you.'

'But how could I have done that?'

'By grassing on the Roxy gang, that's how.'

'Oh look, Mr Heeney, you don't mean it. You gotta be joking. Me grass on you lot! How could I? I didn't know nothing about that warehouse job, and that's God's truth, so it is.'

'So you remember it was a warehouse job?'

'Well, yes. I meanter say—'

'Good memory you got for something that happened all that time ago.'

'Oh, I don't know. It was in the papers, wasn't it? Anybody could've read about it. It was common knowledge.'

'It wasn't common knowledge before it happened. But you knew about it then, didn't you? You kept them big lugs of yours open and you got the breeze, didn't you? And then you passed on the info to Mr Denver, detective inspector as was. So there they was waiting for us, and we was caught with the stuff and didn't stand a snowball's chance in hell of getting off. And it was all because of you, you bloody little grasser.'

Heeney had not raised his voice, because he wanted no one but Lacon to hear what he was saying; but the venom was coming through and the other man was feeling it; his hand shook as he raised the mug to take a mouthful of the beer. He was afraid, and Heeney knew it and noted the fact with satisfaction. He had a score to settle, and this was only the start of it.

'You were Denver's snout, weren't you. You whispered secrets in his ear and he paid you for them. How much did you get for sending me down for all them wasted years. What was the fee for that little bit of Judas work?'

'I—' Lacon began; but no other words escaped from his throat.

'You're scared, aren't you, Lugs?' Heeney said, grinning like a demon. 'And you got reason to be. Because I'm going to make you pay for what you done; just like I'm going to make that swine Denver pay. You both got it coming to you, and it'll come. You're going to pay in full, the pair of you. Do you know what that means – payment in full? Can you guess? Oh yes, I can see you can.'

'You wouldn't,' Lacon said. His voice was a whisper and there was a look of terror in his eyes. 'You wouldn't dare.'

'Like to make a bet on it?' Heeney said.

It was late evening when Denver had a telephone call from an old acquaintance. It was Valerie who answered the telephone, and she came back from the hall to say that the caller was asking to speak to the man of the house.

'He says it's urgent.'

'Did he give his name?'

'No. But he sounded nervous.'

'He wasn't a tout for some double-glazing firm?'

'He didn't say he was. You'd better go and speak to him.'

'All right.' Denver went out to the hall and picked up the telephone. 'Hello! Roy Denver speaking.'

Valerie had been right about the voice coming over the line; it did sound nervous. It also struck a chord in Denver's memory, a chord he would rather not have had touched.

'Oh, Mr Denver, I'm glad you're there. I been trying to get you but there wasn't no answer.'

'I've been out for the evening.' He had in fact been to the theatre with Valerie and had only just come home. 'Who is that speaking?'

'It's me,' the man said. 'You ain't forgotten, have you? Lugs.'

'Ah!' Denver said, sensing trouble and not very happy about it. 'I thought the voice sounded familiar, but it's been a long time. What's on your mind?'

'Plenty. I gotta talk to you, Mr Denver.'

'You are talking to me.'

'Not on the blower, Mr D. I gotta see you.'

'When?'

'Tonight.'

'Oh, I don't know about that,' Denver said. 'It's pretty late.'

'Please, Mr D. For old time's sake.'

There was a note of pleading in Lacon's voice which got through to Denver. Lacon had helped him in the past, and though he had always been paid for the help perhaps he had some claim to consideration. Moreover, Denver was curious to hear what the man had to talk about.

'All right, I'll come straightaway. Where do you want to meet me?'

'The old place?'

'Okay.'

Denver replaced the telephone on its cradle and went back to the living-room. Valerie was far from pleased when he told her that he had to go out again.

'At this time of night! To see that man?'

'Yes.'

'Who is he?'

'His name's Lacon. He used to help me when I was in the CID. Little bits of news about what was going on in the criminal world.'

'You mean he was an informer?'

'That's it.'

'But that was a long time ago. What does he want with you now?'

'I'll know that when I've seen him.'

She was not happy about it, and he was not exactly over the moon himself. But he got the car out and drove to the east side of Rowton Park. It had been raining and the streets were black and shining in the lamplight. He came up quite slowly to the bus shelter, and a dark figure detached itself from the structure amd flitted across to the car and had the door open almost before it had stopped moving.

It was Lacon. He slipped into the passenger seat and pulled the door shut and Denver put the car in motion again.

'You'd better fix your seat-belt,' he said. 'You don't want to have trouble with the law, do you?'

Lacon fastened the seat-belt but said nothing.

'So what's this all about?' Denver asked. 'It had better be important. I'm not a copper any more and I don't fancy being dragged out of a nice comfortable house on a night like this.'

'I've seen Duggie Heeney,' Lacon said. 'He's out.'

'I know. I've seen him, too.'

'I had a talk with him this evening, Mr D.'

'So?'

'He means to kill me.'

'Did he say that?'

'As good as.'

'What precisely did he say?'

'He said he was going to make me pay in full for what I done to get him nicked that time.'

'So he knows it was you who grassed?'

'Yes.'

'And you think payment in full would be your death? That's rather leaping to conclusions, isn't it?'

'I know that's what he meant,' Lacon said; and there was complete conviction in his voice. He leaned towards Denver touching his arm. 'I could tell it was, no mistake. Oh, he meant it all right. He's a nutter and he won't stick at nothing. And he's going to do you too, Mr D.'

'He told you that, did he?'

'Yes. He's got the two of us lined up. I don't know how he got to know I used to work for you and provided the information that led to you putting the grab on him, but it makes no difference. Now he reckons he'll get his own back on both of us.'

Denver was silent, thinking. He wondered why Heeney had given the warning to Lacon, and he thought he could guess the answer. Heeney expected Lacon to come running to him and figured that it would put more of the pressure on. He wanted to make the two of them sweat; it was part of the plan to get his revenge; the psychological part. But it did not mean that he would not get down to the physical measures in the end.

And he was so arrogant, so sure of himself, that he did not hesitate to hand out a warning and put his proposed victims on their guard. It was as if he were contemptuous of anything they might do to protect themselves.

'What are you going to do?' Lacon asked.

'Nothing.'

'Nothing!' Lacon sounded shocked. 'You mean you're just going to sit back and let him get on with it?'

'He won't do anything,' Denver said. 'It's just talk. He wants to scare you, and it looks as if he has.'

'You can bet your back teeth he has. And I don't believe he'll do nothing. You know what he's like.'

'Yes, I know what he's like. But I still don't see what I can do about it, even if he is serious about this business.'

'You gotta help me, Mr D. You owe it to me.'

'I owe you nothing.' Denver spoke sharply. 'Anything you did for me in the past was paid for, and you know it.'

'Maybe so,' Lacon said. 'But I still think you oughter give me a bit of help. I meanter say, if I hadn't given you that tip-off about the Roxy job I wouldn't be in this fix now.'

'Possibly not. But what do you expect me to do?'

'You got friends in the force. You could put a word in, couldn't you?'

'And what good would that do? You expect them to arrest Heeney just because he's breathing down your neck? Or are you looking for police protection? Your own personal bodyguard perhaps? They'd laugh at the idea. Besides which, I doubt whether I have much pull in that department these days. I don't think they'd be falling over themselves to do me any favours.'

Lacon squirmed on his seat. 'So what am I to do? Just wait for him to come and get me?'

It was evident to Denver that Lacon was scared out of his wits. And maybe he did have reason to be. He was probably right about Hecney's being a nut-case, and who could tell what nut-cases might do?

'Well, Lugs,' he said, 'if you really think he means to kill you, I'd say the best thing for you to do would be to scarper.'

'You mean leave Seaport?'

'Why not? What is there to keep you here? You're a free spirit, aren't you? My advice to you is to go to London. It's a big place and he'd never find you there even if he tried. And my guess is he wouldn't try. This is where he operates and this is where he'll stay.'

Lacon seemed doubtful. 'London! Oh, I don't know about that. I've never been there only the once, for the football. Didn't see much of it then, neether. What would I do down there?'

'Same as you're doing here; scratching around.'

Lacon was silent, apparently turning the idea over in his mind and trying it on for size. Then he said: 'Well, if you reckon it's what I oughter do –'

'It's just a suggestion. I'm not trying to persuade you one way or the other. It's up to you to make the decision.'

Which was precisely what Lacon seemed to be finding difficult to do. 'I'm not sure. I've lived here all my life; it's my home. I'm really not sure.'

'Sleep on it,' Denver said. 'In the morning you may find it easier to make up your mind. And now this is where you get off.' He had made the circuit of the park and they were back again at the place where Lacon had joined him. He stopped the car. 'On your way, Lugs.'

Lacon got out of the car and put his head in again. 'How about you, Mr D? Are you going to leave Seaport too?'

'Do you think I should?'

'I think it'd be wise,' Lacon said. 'Because I'd say it's you he's really got it in for. I'm just small fry, but you, Mr D, you're the big fish.'

He shut the door and slunk off into the night like a starving jackal.

The big fish put the car in gear again and drove away, turning those parting words over in his mind and getting precious little comfort from them. Because Lacon could have been right; he could have been dead right at that.

'So what did he want?' Valerie asked.

'Protection,' Denver said. He had driven straight back to the house after getting rid of Lacon.

'Protection! From whom?'

'From Duggie Heeney. That delightful character has been scaring the living daylights out of him. He thinks Heeney is going to kill him.'

'Oh!' she said; and she looked thoughtful and not a little worried. 'And what do you think?'

'I think it's bluff. He won't do anything.'

'You said that before.'

'And I'm still saying it.'

She did a bit more reflecting and then said slowly: 'I'm beginning to see how it is. Lacon was the one who helped you to catch Heeney, wasn't he? And that's why he's come to you for help. Am I right?'

'Well, yes, but –'

'So now this Heeney has a grudge against both of you, and he's threatening Lacon as well as you. Which one will he deal with first, do you think?'

'Neither. I told you, it's just bluff.'

'Lacon obviously doesn't think so.'

'He'd be scared of his own shadow.'

'That doesn't mean he might not be right. Are you going to help him?'

'I can't. I advised him to go to London.'

'Because of a piece of bluff?'

'Because he thinks it's more than bluff. It would ease his mind.'

After a while she said: 'You think it's more than bluff, too, don't you? Really.'

'No,' he said. 'No, I don't.' But he could tell that she did not believe him. And he knew that she was right.

FOURTEEN
Too Smart

Heeney read a report in the paper about a shooting that had occurred at a big country house called Earlington Grange, which was about twenty miles from Seaport. It appeared to have been quite a gun battle, and by the time the police arrived on the scene there were five dead men in various parts of the house, two others badly injured and a lot of blood on the carpets.

The theory was that it had been a fight between two gangs of criminals, and what lent weight to this idea was the discovery of a considerable quantity of heroin with an estimated street value of some two million pounds. A search of the estate revealed further gruesome evidence in the shape of two more bodies buried in a wood. Each of these dead men had also been shot.

Heeney grinned; he found it all highly amusing. Because it took no great powers of deduction to guess why the fight had taken place. When the two men who were taking the suitcases of money to buy the heroin failed to return from the trip, their confederates had quickly jumped to the conclusion that there had been a rip-off. So they had gone to the Grange with guns to put the record straight. And then there had probably been an argument and tempers had been lost and the shooting had started.

141

It was all very funny, Heeney thought; it really made him laugh. But what he found not quite so funny was that mention of two million pounds. Just how much had Mr G raked in from those two locked suitcases? It made him far from satisfied with his share of the loot. Ten thousand pounds was all very well, but it was only one hundredth of a million and was certainly not riches.

And after all, he was the one who had killed the two men in the car, and he reckoned he should have had some kind of bonus for that. All in all he felt pretty disgruntled, and next time he would certainly demand a bigger cut, whether Mr G liked it or not. He was not going to work for peanuts.

He had given his mother fifty pounds. 'Buy yourself a new hat.'

She looked at the money and then at him. 'You got a job then, Duggie?'

'Something of the sort.'

She seemed inclined to ask more questions, but the expression on his face stopped her. She put the money in a vase on the sideboard in the living-room.

'Thanks, Duggie. You're a good boy. You think about your old mum.'

Heeney grinned at her. If only she knew what he thought about the old haybag! But she had her uses.

Lugs Lacon spent a restless night after his talk in the car with Denver. Not that this was at all unusual, because he was not living in the most luxurious of quarters and sometimes when it rained hard a certain amount of leakage found its way on to his bed and ruined his slumbers.

The bed was in fact nothing better than a lumpy old mattress which he had picked up from a rubbish dump and had installed in a ramshackle hut on an abandoned allotment. It was in this hut that he had, quite illegally, established himself after having been thrown out of his previous accommodation, a seedy bed-sitter, for non-payment of rent.

Lacon was one of society's casualties; he was living from hand to mouth, and sometimes he had serious thoughts of committing some petty crime like throwing a brick through a shop window just to get himself arrested and sent back to prison. But so far he had lacked the courage to take such a deliberate step and had continued to hang on in his wretched little shack, hoping against hope that something good would one day turn up.

This had always been improbable to say the least, since he had no rich relations who might die and leave him a pot of gold and no premium bonds which might bring in a cool quarter of a million. Instead, what did turn up was a character named Duggie Heeney with an old score to settle. And now even the allotment hut no longer seemed like a haven of safety, because there were too many people who knew where his refuge was, and might not Heeney discover it also?

So as the dragging hours of the night slowly crept away he became more and more sold on that idea of Denver's that he should quit Seaport and travel south to London. There was, of course, one snag: he had less than a pound in hard cash, and rail or bus tickets to London cost the devil of a lot these days. He regretted now that he had not asked Denver for a hand-out when they were having their discussion the previous evening; but perhaps it was still not too late to pick up his rail fare from that source, and maybe a little extra besides to give him a start in the Metropolis. If he went up to the house early enough he ought to be able to catch Denver before he went off to whatever job he was engaged on.

Before dawn Lacon had reached a decision: he would leave Seaport and he would try to get some help from Denver in the financial line. With this project in mind he rose from the old mattress as soon as a little grey morning light began to filter into the hut by way of the polythene-covered window and set about packing his meagre possessions into an ancient and battered suitcase.

He reflected as he did so that there was little enough that he had gathered in the course of some fifty-six years of existence on the planet earth; it had, when all was said and done, been a pretty futile life and gave promise of nothing better in the future. Some people might have maintained that it had no value whatever and was not worth clinging to; and yet the very possibility of losing it filled him with horror. It was illogical but it was nevertheless a fact. He did not wish to die.

He was tying the suitcase with a length of cord because the catches were broken when he heard a sound outside. His heart seemed to skip a beat, and then the door was pulled open and Heeney stepped inside and closed it behind him.

'Well, well, well!' Heeney said, glancing at the suitcase. 'Looks like I was only just in time. Lucky me! A little later and you'd have pulled out. You wasn't planning to give me the slip, was you, Lugs?'

Lacon felt trapped. He saw now that he should have got away while it was still dark. Heeney had been too smart for him and had come at the crack of dawn, before anyone but the earliest of birds was stirring. Maybe he had had a suspicion that Lacon might make a run for it after their talk in the public-house, and so had decided to act without delay.

'Have you been talking to Denver?' Heeney asked. 'Did he advise you to clear out?'

Lacon wondered how Heeney could have made such a shrewd guess. He was smart, no doubt about that.

'Did you tell him what I said to you?' Heeney asked. 'About payment in full.'

Lacon found his voice, though it sounded hardly like his own. 'Yes, I told him. He said it was bluff.'

'Do you think it was?'

'I don't know.'

'But you hope it was, don't you?'

'Yes,' Lacon said. What else could he say? It was his only hope.

Heeney laughed. Lacon noticed that he was wearing black leather gloves; he wondered whether there was any significance in this.

'Does this look like bluff?' Heeney asked. He put a hand inside his jacket and pulled out a knife. It was the sort that could be found in any number of kitchens, black-handled, with a pointed razor-edged blade about eight inches long. He showed it to Lacon, holding it lightly in his hand, the point directed towards Heeney's stomach. 'What do you think now?'

Lacon stared at the knife as if mesmerised. 'No!' he whispered. 'No, Duggie, no!'

Heeney grinned at him, savagely, pitilessly. 'Yes!' he said. 'Yes, Lugs, yes!'

FIFTEEN

Not in Favour

'It was Duggie Heeney,' Denver said. 'It had to be him.'

Detective Chief Inspector Rufford looked at him sourly. 'Do you have proof of that?'

Denver remembered that Rufford had been a sergeant when he himself had been an inspector, and there had been friction between them then. He guessed that Rufford would not take kindly to any interference on his part in the present case and might even treat any suggestions from him with less than the seriousness they deserved simply because of the source from which they came.

The body of Lugs Lacon had been discovered not many hours after the murder had taken place, which made it possible for the police surgeon to make a fairly confident estimate of the time of death. A man who knew Lacon well and had been in the habit of looking in on him on his way to work had come upon the bloodstained corpse soon after eight o'clock in the morning. He said it had given him a nasty shock, and there was no reason to doubt this statement. He had touched nothing but had called the police without delay.

It had not been until several hours later that Denver had heard of the killing. He had got in touch with the Seaport CID and had been referred to Detective Chief Inspector Charles Rufford, who was working on the

147

case. Rufford had greeted him with a singular lack of cordiality when he had eventually caught up with the chief inspector at the mortuary.

However, Rufford did permit him to take a look at the body on the slab, and Denver was able to corroborate that the dead man was indeed Lugs Lacon; the ears alone were unmistakable. It appeared that Lacon had been killed with just one thrust to the heart with a knife, but the weapon had not been found.

'No proof, no,' Denver admitted. 'Just evidence.'

'What evidence?'

'Heeney had been threatening Lacon. He said he was going to deal with him first and then me.'

Rufford treated Denver to a hard look. 'Who told you that?'

'Lacon. We had a talk yesterday evening in my car. He was scared and he wanted help.'

'Why come to you? Why not to us?'

'Well, you know what he was like. He used to be my snout in the old days. He was the one who gave me the tip-off that led to Heeney's arrest. Now Heeney's out again he's making it his business to take revenge on the people mainly concerned with putting him inside: Lacon and me.'

'And it was Lacon who told you all this?'

'Yes.'

'So you've only got his word for this revenge story?'

'No. I had a talk with Heeney himself, earlier.'

'And he threatened to kill you?'

'Not in so many words. He was careful not to go that far. It was all hints and nudges, but the message was crystal clear.'

Rufford stroked his long pointed chin and shook his head in admonition. 'You should have come to us with this information. You both should. It would have been the proper thing to do. You of all people, as an ex-police officer, ought to have known that.'

'What good would it have done? Heeney would have denied it, and there was nothing in writing, no proof.'

'Maybe not; but we should have been told. And there's no proof now, either. Not even any real evidence. Just something he's supposed to have said to Lacon and something he said to you. It doesn't amount to much, does it?'

'I suppose it doesn't. But I still think you ought to question him. He did have a motive.'

'We have questioned him,' Rufford said.

'Oh!' It took the wind out of Denver's sails. He had to admit that Rufford had been a good deal quicker off the mark than he had imagined.

'We're not all boneheads since you left, you know. We spotted the connection between Heeney and Lacon at once, because we knew Lugs used to work for you. It was obvious that the murder couldn't have been done for motives of robbery; all he had was in an old suitcase he'd packed as if he'd intended leaving but was too late. So we went along to Heeney's mother's flat and found him there and had a talk.'

'With what result?'

'Negative. He's got an alibi. His mother says she got up at six o'clock and he was still in bed. He wasn't out of the sack till nine, when he had his breakfast, and he'd been in the flat ever since.'

'It's what he told her to say, of course.'

'Possibly. But we can't prove that.'

'Did you search the flat?'

'Yes. We didn't have a warrant but neither of them raised any objection. Guess what we found.'

'Nothing?'

'Right in one. Not a thing to incriminate him.'

'No fingerprints at the scene of the crime?'

'Only Lacon's and those of the man who found him; and they were just on the door.'

'Clever devil, Heeney. Wonder what he did with the

knife.'

'We're looking for the murder weapon,' Rufford said, 'but frankly I don't think we'll find it.'

Denver was of the same opinion; Heeney would have got rid of it far away from the place where the killing had been committed; he was no fool. So it looked as though he was going to get away with murder. And maybe it was not the first time, either.

Valerie was already home when he got back to the house. He had to tell her what had happened, though he knew it would worry her; she would have got to know eventually anyway.

'Oh God!' she said. 'So he's killed Lacon and now you'll be the next.'

'It doesn't follow.'

'Of course it follows.' She sounded impatient. 'Don't try to fob me off with soothing words. You know as well as I do that this killing just goes to prove he wasn't bluffing. So now he's got Lacon out of the way he'll turn his attention to you. He will, won't he?'

Denver saw that it would be pointless to deny it; he could no longer hope to convince her that he was in no danger from the ex-convict.

'Yes, I imagine he will.'

'Do the police know this? Did you tell them he threatened you?'

'Yes, I told Rufford.'

'And what's he going to do to protect you?'

'Nothing.'

'Nothing! But he must. He can't just stand by and let it happen.'

'What do you expect him to do? Give me round-the-clock police protection, a guard on the house? I'm not a VIP; I don't rate that kind of attenion. To a certain extent I dare say they'll keep an eye on Heeney, but mostly it'll be up to me to be on my guard and not give him the chance to get at me.'

'That may be easier said than done.'

He needed no one to point this out to him. Heeney could afford to bide his time and wait for the opportunity to strike. And however careful you were you could not always be on the alert; it was not humanly possible.

'Perhaps you should go away for a time,' Valerie suggested.

Denver shook his head. 'That's no good. I'd have to come back eventually, and he'd still be here. And what about the business? I can't just leave it; I have to make a living. Besides which, I'm damned if I'll run away from a swine like Duggie Heeney.'

'You'd rather be killed, I suppose.'

'Damn it!' he said, beginning to lose his temper. 'I'm not going to be killed. Put that idea right out of your mind once and for all.'

She sighed. 'If only I could.'

Later she told him that Kenneth Roper wanted her to go to London with him for two or three days. Denver was instantly suspicious of her employer's motive.

'Oh, he does, does he?'

'You needn't say it like that,' she snapped. 'I know what you're thinking, but you're wrong. It's a purely business trip; he's going to a conference and he'd like me to be on hand.'

'Why?'

'Because he may need some secretarial work done, of course. What else?'

'I don't know what else, do I?' Denver said. But he remembered his talk with Roper and he would have made a guess that the boss of Micro Plastics regarded Miss West not solely as a very efficient private secretary but also as a most desirable young woman. Therefore he regarded with considerable lack of enthusiasm the proposed excursion to the bright lights of the capital city. 'When is he planning to go?'

'Thursday.'

'The day after tomorrow! That's pretty short notice, isn't it? How long have you known about this?'

'It's been in his diary for some time, of course; but he didn't tell me until today that he wanted me to go with him.'

'So it was a brilliant idea that suddenly came into his mind?'

'That would be one way of putting it, I suppose. Do I get the impression that you're not altogether in favour?'

'Damn right, you do. Why would I be in favour? I like having you here, not gadding around with the Whizzkid.'

'You promised not to call him that any more,' she said sharply. 'And I'll not be gadding around with him, as you so sweetly put it. I'll just be doing my job.'

'And after the day's work is done?'

'What precisely do you mean by that?' she asked, with a lift of the eyebrows.

'No relaxation? Nightclubs, dancing, that kind of thing. With a handsome partner.'

'My God!' she said. 'You're jealous, aren't you? You're just plain jealous. Maybe you think I'm going to sleep with him.'

'I think it could be what he has in mind.'

'Oh, for heaven's sake! Is that what's bothering you? Is that how much you trust me? Well, now we know, don't we? This certainly does clear the air.'

She was really angry now, and he could see that it was developing into a stand-up fight. Which was something he surely did not want. As if he didn't have enough on his mind already with this Duggie Heeney business! He decided to cool it.

'I'm sorry, Val. I shouldn't have said that. Of course I trust you. And maybe it'll be good for you to have a break. I'll manage all right for a few days on my own. It's not as though you were going away for a month or a year, is it? I shall miss you, of course, but I'll live through it.'

The last few words seemed to touch a nerve, and in a sudden change of mood she reached out and took his hand in hers. 'I'm not sure now that I ought to go. I'll be worrying all the time about you, wondering whether that awful man has carried out his threat.'

'Now that's stupid,' Denver said. 'Of course you must go. Nothing's going to happen to me while you're away. I promise.'

'Well,' she said, 'I'll think about it. I love you, Roy.'

'I love you too, Val.'

She laughed. 'Well, at least we've got that settled, haven't we?'

SIXTEEN

Bait

It was almost five o'clock the next day when Valerie West arrived home. She brought the Mini to a halt on the gravel at the front of the house and had unfastened the seat-belt and opened the door but was still in the car when a man suddenly appeared as if from nowhere.

'Don't get out, Miss West,' he said. He came up close to the half-opened door and she saw that he had a knife in his hand. 'You and me's got some business to talk about.'

She had never seen him before, but she knew in an instant that he was Douglas Heeney; it could have been no one else. And she was afraid. The knife was perhaps the very one that had killed Lacon, or another one; it made no difference; either way it was lethal.

Heeney had been waiting at the back of the house for more than an hour, and he had made sure that there was no one else around. When he had heard the Mini coming up the drive he had crept round to the front, keeping close to the wall, and had noted with satisfaction that it was Miss West returning. Since seeing her on that first occasion he had made some discreet inquiries and had to got know her name and where she worked. Now he intended making use of her in the plan he had in mind. It was all working right for him, just as he wanted it to.

'What do you want with me?' she asked, trying, not very successfully, to keep the tremor out of her voice. 'Who are you?'

'Don't you know?' He spoke mockingly. 'Haven't you guessed? My name's Heeney. Don't say Mr Denver's never mentioned me to you.'

She said nothing. He was merely confirming that her conjecture had been correct. It gave her no feeling of satisfaction to realise that this was so.

'Open the other door and fasten your seat-belt,' Heeney said. 'We're going for a nice little ride.'

She made no immediate move to obey him, but he gave her a prick with the point of the knife and snarled at her to do what she was told. She had no choice, for she knew that he would not have hesitated to inflict more than a mere prick with the knife if she made any resistance. So she opened the door and fastened the belt.

Heeney ran round to the other side of the car and got in. He was still holding the knife in his hand.

'Now shut your door and start her up.'

She did so.

'Turn the car and let's be on our way.'

She did that, too. At the gateway he told her to turn to the left, and after that he directed her as she drove, always keeping the knife ready for use if she should prove recalcitrant.

'You're doing nicely,' he said. 'Keep it like that and maybe you won't get hurt. But don't think up any smart ideas in that pretty little head of yours, because if you try anything clever you could grab yourself a nasty injury. You understand, lady?'

'I understand,' she said.

'Good.'

She had in fact had vague thoughts of stopping the car if she saw a policeman and maybe making a dash for it. But she would never have been able to get out fast enough, and even under the very eyes of the law she knew there was no certainty that Heeney would not dare to use the knife. From what Roy had told her she had gathered that the man was practically a psychopath, and as such was completely unpredictable in his actions.

The way he was directing her indicated that they were heading towards the river and the old docks area; but before they reached that part of the town he gave her the order to take a left-hand turning and after a time they came to one of the districts where the recession had had its worst effect. Here there were boarded-up shops and crumbling houses and stretches of waste ground on which stood derelict factory buildings, with rank weeds and stunted thorn bushes and elder trees and brambles that had established themselves in the thin and impoverished soil.

Heeney directed Miss West to drive the car into a cul-de-sac where the houses on each side were empty, windows broken and sheets of corrugated iron blocking doorways from which the doors themselves had probably been taken for use as firewood.

'Stop here,' he said.

She did so and switched off the engine. Heeney took the keys and got out. He walked round to Miss West's side and tapped on the glass.

'Get out.'

She released the seat-belt and got out of the car. She thought of making off at a run down the cul-de-sac, but there was not a soul in sight who might have helped her and she was afraid Heeney would have overtaken her before she had gone a dozen paces; there was a lean greyhoundish look about him.

So she did not move as he locked the car and pocketed the keys. He had stowed the knife away under his jacket, but she had no doubt that he could have whipped it out in a moment if the necessity had arisen. He gripped her right arm just above the elbow.

'Come along now.'

There was an alleyway between the houses at the end of the cul-de-sac, and he must have been there before, since he appeared to know exactly where he was going. At the end of the alleyway they came out on to some of that ravaged landscape such as she had already seen from the car, and Heeney pushed her through a gap in a fence and followed close behind. Then he took hold of her arm again.

It was one of those late summer or early autumn days when a touch of November seems to have made a premature arrival. The sky was murky and the rough grass underfoot was already damp from the light precipitation that was something midway between a heavy mist and a light drizzle. Visibility was poor, and Miss West could see no one on this expanse of desolate ground; she was alone with the psychopath. It was not the most cheering of situations.

Although she had no means of knowing it, this was in fact another part of that same piece of wasteland on which Heeney had had his encounter with the three skinheads, and it was not very far distant from the block of flats where he was now living with his mother. It was a wilderness which the police only occasionally visited and where in various ways the law was flouted with impunity.

Valerie West, stumbling along with Heeney in close attendance, had an increasing sense of dread. In this misty desolation she saw no hope of anyone coming to her aid, and she had good reason, knowing what kind of man she had to deal with, to fear what he might be proposing to do with her. And it was of no use appealing to his better nature, since he almost certainly had none; he was one of those criminals who were entirely lacking in the restraint of any kind of morality.

'Where are you taking me?' she asked.

'You'll see,' Heeney said.

What eventually she did see was a gaunt derelict building that no doubt had once hummed with industry but was now dead and silent. A crumbling monument to a vanished prosperity. Heeney dragged her into the gloomy interior from which the machinery had long since been stripped and which was now no more than an abandoned shell. There was a chill in the air, and the vast empty space produced an eerie echo of the sound of their footfalls and their voices.

'Like it?' Heeney asked. 'One large desirable residence in need of a bit of renovation. You'll be very comfortable here, I'm sure.'

He was mocking her, taunting. He had released her arm and was standing a yard or two away from her, staring at her as though, now that he had the time to spare, he were making a careful assessment of her appearance. She stared back at him fearfully, detecting no hint of pity in his eyes.

'Yes,' he said, 'you're not a bad-looker, not bad at all. I'd say you're a sight too good for that bastard Denver. Come to think of it, I wouldn't mind having you myself. What would you say to that? You could do worse.'

He leered at her, and she was only too well aware that she was entirely in his power. She could feel the chill coming up from the concrete floor through the soles of her shoes, and she shivered.

'Why have you brought me here?' she asked. 'What are you intending to do with me?'

Heeney grinned. 'Why,' he said, 'I do believe you're scared. You don't need to be; you're not the one I got an account to settle with. I don't have nothing against you, lady, except maybe the fact that you're living with Mr Bloody Denver; loving and cherishing him, as they say. But he's the one I really want.'

'So why —'

'Why've I put the snatch on you? The answer's simple. You're bait.'

'Bait?'

'That's it. You're a sprat to catch a mackerel, and he's the mackerel. Now do you see?'

She did see. Heeney was going to use her to entice Roy on to ground of his own choosing. But would the intended victim walk into the trap?

'How much would you say he loves you?' Heeney asked. 'I hope it's a lot. I hope it's enough for him to put hisself on the line for your sake. And you better hope so too, else I don't see you getting out of this alive.'

Her eyes widened. 'You wouldn't kill me! What good would that do?'

Heeney shrugged. 'Well, it's up to him. You better just hope he does things the right way.'

There was a lump of wood lying on the floor not far from where Heeney was standing. Casually he walked across and picked it up before strolling back to his former position. Miss West watched him, not moving. She could have made a run for it when his attention had wandered away from her, but she lacked the will. It was as though the man had hypnotised her and she had become subservient to his will.

He hefted the piece of wood in his hand, glancing at her reflectively. Still she did not stir, but simply watched the movement of the cudgel in his hand. It was two inches thick and about a foot long. Suddenly he took a step forward and struck her with it.

She had seen the blow coming and had jerked away from it; but she was too late. The cudgel caught her on the side of the head. She felt the crushing impact of the wood and nothing more.

SEVENTEEN
Not Smart Enough

Denver had just arrived home when the telephone rang. Valerie was apparently not in, so he had to answer it himself. He lifted the receiver and a man started speaking at the other end of the line without waiting for him to say a word.

'That you, Mr Denver?' The voice sounded vaguely familiar but he could not quite place it.

'Yes,' he said, 'this is Roy Denver.'

'Good. Glad I caught you in.'

'You nearly didn't. I've only just got home.'

The caller gave a chuckle, which somehow managed to convey the impression that he was feeling highly pleased with himself. 'To an empty house and all. Too bad.'

'How did you –' Denver began; and it was as though an icy hand had suddenly clutched at his heart. 'Who is that speaking?'

'Don't you know? Can't you guess, Inspector?'

He got it then. 'Heeney!'

'Right in one. None other.'

'What did you mean by saying I'd come home to an empty house?'

'Why, nothing, Mr Denver, nothing at all. Except that it wasn't likely there'd be anybody to welcome you with open loving arms, seeing as how Miss West's not there.'

'Damn you, Heeney!' Denver burst out; and the hand with its icy fingers was clutching tighter now, hurting. 'What do you know about Miss West?'

Heeney chuckled again; he surely was pleased with himself, no doubt about it. 'More than you'd think. I know where she is, see. I know where that little white Mini is and all.'

'What sort of game are you playing at?' Denver demanded. But he knew.

'No game,' Heeney said. 'No kid's stuff this. It's dead serious. You know what I'm talking about, don't you?'

'No. You'd better tell me.'

'I'm talking about you doing just exactly what I tell you to do; else you might never see that sweet little lady alive again. Never. Got it?'

Denver had some difficulty in replying coherently; he was so choked with anger and frustration. He wanted to get at Heeney and strangle him; but Heeney was out of reach, and he was safe anyway because he had a hostage. Denver had to do as he was told and not put a foot wrong, because the likely consequence of any slip was too horrible to contemplate.

'Yes,' he said; the word seeming to stick in his gullet, so that it finally came out with a coughing sound as though he were clearing phlegm.

'Good. Now listen carefully; this is what you have to do. Are you listening?'

'Damn you!' Denver said again. 'Of course I'm listening. What else would I be doing?' He knew that Heeney was tormenting him by purposely making the business as long drawn out as possible. And he certainly was tormented, because he could not rid his mind of the picture of Valerie in Heeney's filthy hands. What had the bastard done to her and with her? He had never wanted to kill anybody as badly as he wanted to kill Heeney at that moment. But he had to remain calm; it was essential. 'Tell me what you want me to do.'

'There's a place you gotta come to,' Heeney said. 'I'll tell you how to get there. Maybe you better write the directions down so's you don't forget.'

'I won't forget,' Denver said. He knew Seaport from one end to the other; it had been his job to know. 'Just tell me where I'm to meet you.'

'Here, hold on,' Heeney said. 'Who said anything about you meeting me?'

'Well, for Christ's sake! Isn't that the whole object of the exercise? You've snatched Miss West to make me come to you in some place where you fancy you'll have the advantage over me. That's what it's all about, isn't it?'

Heeney answered sulkily: 'You're so smart, Inspector; you really are.'

'Not smart enough to prevent you getting the drop on me, it seems.'

'That's true.'

'So now why don't you tell me where it is I have to go?'

Heeney told him. 'But be sure to come alone and don't bring a shooter. Above all, don't tell the coppers. You bring them in and Miss West's a goner. You can count on that. This is strictly between you and me; no interference.'

'All right. You're calling the tune,' Denver said.

And yet he knew as well as anyone could know that the sensible and proper course for him now was to call the police immediately and tell them that Heeney had kidnapped Miss West. He knew from experience that it was the regular thing for kidnappers to warn the people they were putting the pressure on not to bring in officers of the law; and all too often those people were so scared of putting the victim's life in jeopardy that they obeyed the instructions. Yet it was undoubtedly the wrong way to deal with the situation; the police were trained to handle such cases, and failure to call them in at the outset could lead to disastrous consequences.

Denver had been a policeman himself and he knew that this was true. And yet when it came to the point, when he himself was at the receiving end of the operation, he hesitated, wondering whether this might perhaps be the exceptional case which it would be better for him to handle on his own, keeping it to a personal battle between himself and Heeney without the involvement of any outsiders.

So when Heeney had rung off he remained with his hand on the telephone, still undecided, unable to make up his mind regarding what course of action to take. But all his former training was urging him powerfully to enlist the aid of his one-time colleagues, and finally he lifted the receiver again and dialled a number. Within a few seconds he got a reply, a man's voice inviting him to state his problem.

But it was Heeney who seemed to be speaking, telling him that if he did anything out of line he would never see Valerie alive again; and he stood there with the instrument in his hand, saying nothing, doing nothing, not moving. Perhaps he would never again see her alive anyway; perhaps she was already dead. But he could not be sure, and until he was sure he must do nothing that might possibly increase the threat to her.

The voice at the other end of the line was saying something: 'Hello! Are you there, caller? Hello!'

He put the receiver down and silenced the voice.

It was perfectly obvious to him what Heeney's plan was because it was so simple. The snatch of Miss Valerie West had been carried out with the sole purpose of luring him to the old factory building which Heeney had described in his instructions. There the man intended to kill him as he had already killed Lacon; there could be no other reason for what he was doing. So, in going to the rendezvous, he, Denver, would be walking into the trap and putting his own life on the line. Of that there could be no doubt whatever.

Yet it was ridiculous to imagine that he could save the woman by sacrificing himself; that was a dream, a fantasy. The forfeit of his life would be a futile gesture serving no conceivable useful purpose. For it was as certain as night following day that, even if Valerie were not already dead, Heeney would kill her as soon as he had dealt with his other victim.

Denver knew that he was on a hiding to nothing; but he had to go; there was no question in his mind about that. He had to play the game Heeney's way and just trust that somehow or other he could snatch something from the fire. If he had possessed a gun he might have ignored Heeney's warning and taken it along with him nevertheless; but he did not have one. He thought of taking a knife but rejected the idea; he was not a knife-fighter and had always condemned the use of such a weapon, the favoured implement of thugs and hooligans, whom he despised.

As he hesitated the minutes were ticking away. Well, there was nothing for it but to go; there would be no advantage in delay and it would be advisable to get to the rendezvous while there was still some daylight remaining. In darkness Heeney would certainly have the advantage.

Not that he would not have it anyway.

The light was already none too good when he left his car and set out on foot for the last part of the way. The mist had eventually transformed itself into a genuine drizzle of rain and the cloud cover was hastening the approach of darkness. Denver was wearing a gaberdine zip-up jacket, but he was bare-headed and his hair was soon wet and dripping. It was indeed well that he was familiar with the area, otherwise he might have had considerable difficulty in finding the building to which Heeney had directed him. As it was he had to be careful where he set his feet because of the many holes and other hazards that beset the way, and it was not long before he became aware of an unpleasant sogginess in his shoes.

He met no one; and this fact did not surprise him, since it was unlikely that anyone would be taking a stroll for pleasure in the prevailing conditions. Only someone like himself who had urgent business to attend to in those surroundings would have ventured into this dismal wasteland, and he doubted whether there was anyone else except Douglas Heeney who did have any business there.

Eventually he caught sight of a shadowy grey mass looming out of the murk ahead and knew that he was approaching the place of meeting and the final showdown. His pulse quickened and he could feel his heart thumping. He could not control this reaction; knowing that when he walked into that building he would find a man waiting to kill him, it would have required superhuman self-control to have remained perfectly calm and composed. Denver had never made any claim to being more than a fairly ordinary mortal and he was as fearful of death as the next man. He was certainly not the fearless hero of legend, and he suspected that in real life the only people who came into that category were those who lacked the intelligence to appreciate what danger was. Idiots, in fact. Well, he was no idiot and he was scared; that was certain. But it was also certain that he was not scared enough to be petrified by the feeling: he would do what he had to do in spite of it.

When he approached more closely he could discern a doorway, and he moved towards it with caution. As he did so he heard a kind of scuffling sound away to his right and he glanced quickly in that direction. It might have been a trick of the light, but he thought he caught a glimpse of something moving near the corner of the building; but it was only momentary, a shadow that might perhaps have been there but was gone before it could be identified as anything more substantial.

He came to a halt, wondering whether there had in fact been anything or whether an over-active sensitivity on his part had made him imagine something where there was nothing. Yet there had been a sound; he felt sure of that even if he could not be certain of what he might or might not have seen. So maybe he ought to go and investigate. He hesitated, undecided whether to do so or not; but finally he gave a shrug and walked through the doorway.

Inside the building the drizzle no longer descended on to his head and shoulders: this was the only advantage that could be detected. It was still as cold and dismal as it had been outside, and the light was no better. Denver let his gaze wander round the vast deserted interior and could see no sign of Heeney.

So perhaps it had been Heeney who had made that faint scuffling noise outside and had been the shadow half-glimpsed from the corner of the eye. Perhaps at this very moment he was preparing to slip silently in and take his victim from the rear.

Denver swung round to face the doorway, but no one was there. He was getting jumpy, and that would never do. He had to be on the alert but not like a cat on hot bricks.

He gave a shout: 'Heeney! Where are you?'

The sound of his voice echoed hollowly, coming back at him off the bare walls; but there was no other answer. What was the man doing? Was he there or was he not? Was it all a game he was playing, bringing Denver out there on a wild-goose chase while he himself was somewhere else?

And Valerie too! Where was she?

He took a few more steps, bringing himself nearer the centre of the building, and then stopped again.

'Heeney! What in hell are you playing at? Are you there, damn you?'

Again he received no reply but the echoes. He started walking again, moving towards the far end of the interior. There were piles of junk lying here and there – bits of old iron, a few bricks, chunks of plaster. He made his way to the end wall, turned and looked back. It was so gloomy now that he could scarcely see the opposite end; it was in heavy shadow.

He was now in a quandary: if Heeney was not there it was pointless to hang around. Could it be that he had made a mistake and come to the wrong building? It was possible, but he felt sure this was the one that Heeney had directed him to. Still, if the man was not anywhere about there was nothing he could do to contact him. It was all damned frustrating. What was he to do?

He began moving back the way he had come, taking it slowly and still on the alert, when suddenly he heard a laugh and then Heeney's mocking voice.

'Thought I wasn't here, didn't you, Mr Denver? Well, you were wrong; I'm here all right, you bet your life I am.'

Denver caught sight of him then. There was an iron ladder leading up to a kind of gallery at that end of the building which he was now facing, and at the head of the ladder he could just make out the shape of a man. Heeney was leaning on a rail and looking down. He must have been concealed up there when Denver had walked in and had been amusing himself at the expense of the newcomer. But now he had come out into the open and things would begin to happen.

EIGHTEEN

Lamb to the Slaughter

'So you've been playing hide-and-seek with me,' Denver said.

'That's about it. Now stop right where you are and I'll come down to you.'

Denver halted about fifteen paces from the foot of the ladder. Heeney came down nimbly, one hand on a side-rail. He advanced a yard or two and took a good look at Denver.

'So you came then. You really came.'

'Yes, I came,' Denver said. 'What did you expect me to do?'

'I did just wonder,' Heeney said. 'I asked myself if you'd really be such a bonehead as to walk straight into it, all for the sake of a judy. No, I said to myself, he won't do it; he's got too much savvy for that; he'll stay away; he won't put himself in my hands just on the chance he might be able to help his bit of skirt get out of the mess she's dropped in; it's too much to expect. That's what I said, because really it looked like an awful long shot that you'd be so bloody daft. But I was wrong, wasn't I?'

'Yes, you were wrong.'

'So I was. And of course that's what I was counting on in the first place; that you really had lost your marbles over this here Miss Valerie West and wouldn't act like

the clever cop you once was. You've gone soft since
them days, Inspector, real soft. Who'd of thought it?'

'Cut the cackle,' Denver said. 'Where is she?'

Heeney grinned slyly. 'Now wouldn't you just like to
know! Because if you don't get to know that, there was
no sense in coming, was there? From your point of view,
I mean. Not that there was any sense in it anyway,
seeing as how I'm going to kill you, you bastard. That's
what I got you here for, and you know it, don't you?'

'I know you'll try to kill me,' Denver said. 'It remains
to be seen whether or not you'll manage it.' He
wondered whether Heeney had a pistol hidden away,
but he doubted it. He had used a knife to kill Lacon, and
the odds were that he was planning to use the same
method this time.

'I'll manage it,' Heeney said. He sounded confident;
quite cocky in fact. 'Just whenever I please.'

Denver thought of rushing him before he could get
the weapon out; but Heeney was wary and the distance
between the two of them was too great.

'It was you who killed Lugs, of course?'

'How right you are. It was easy. No trouble at all. And
him just packing to go.'

'How many people have you killed altogether,
Duggie?'

'Do you really want to know?'

'Yes. As a matter of interest.'

'As a matter of interest, then; five. You'll be number
six.'

'A proper little killer, aren't you? And you've always
got away with it, too.'

'That's because I'm bright.'

'You're not bright,' Denver said. 'You're a nut-case.
You're wrong in the head. So far you've been lucky, but
the luck won't last for ever. It could be running out on
you right now.'

'Shut your mouth,' Heeney shouted. It was evident

that Denver's words had touched him on the raw. 'There's nothing wrong inside my head; it's as good as yours, and better. I got you here, didn't I? So that means I'm cleverer than you. I got you where I want you.'

'Maybe you have,' Denver said.'Maybe you've worked it right. But there's still one thing I'd like to know. What have you done with Miss West?'

'So you're still on about that. I told you it wouldn't do you no good to know. You can't help her.'

'All the same, I'd like you to tell me. And why not? What would you lose by telling?'

Heeney shook his head. 'No; it's no use. I'm not going to give you that satisfaction. You're going to snuff it without even knowing if she's dead or alive; without knowing if I've carved her up or raped her or anything. She's a nice lady, that one, pretty as a picture. I reckon you really enjoy being in bed with her. Or should I say you did enjoy it? Because it's all over now; no more of that for you, Inspector; not after this. Still, you can't grumble; you was having the best things in life while I was doing time in Parkways because of you. But now that's all changed and I've got the whiphand. And when I've finished with you it's me as can go and do what I like with the judy. She's mine now, all mine; every last bit of her.'

It was only with a superhuman effort of will that Denver managed to keep control of himself. Under Heeney's taunting he had become possessed by such an overpowering rage that he wanted to rush at the man and smash that leering face to pulp with his clenched fists. But he knew that he would have been met by the knife that was surely there, just waiting for Heeney's fingers to grasp the handle and bring it out. The weapon was hidden now but it would appear in a moment when the need to use it arose.

'Still,' Heeney said, 'I'll be generous; I'll give you a chance. Can't say fairer than that, can I?'

Denver looked at him, suspecting duplicity in the

offer. He did not believe Heeney's words; the swine wanted his pound of flesh and he meant to take it whatever happened.

'Chance! What chance?'

'We'll fight it out. Winner takes all. And that includes the lady.'

'Have you changed your mind, then? Are you going to tell me where she is before we start?'

'No.'

'So what happens if I kill you? How do I find her?

'You'll have to search for her, won't you? But you won't kill me. I'm going to kill you.'

'This fight,' Denver said; 'is it to be on equal terms?'

Heeney laughed. 'We'll each fight with what we've got. Did you bring a gun?'

'No.'

'I thought not. You'd have had it out by now, threatening me. How about a knife?'

'No knife either.'

'I'm surprised. You're pretty stupid really. You just walk straight into it like a lamb to the slaughter.'

'And you're the butcher?'

'What do you think this looks like?'

Heeney's hand dived under his jacket and came out with a long pointed butcher's knife. It was a good enough answer to the question.

He came at Denver then. The formalities were finished and the fight was on. Or maybe the execution.

There was a lump of concrete lying near Denver's right foot; he had noticed it when he had come to a halt. Now, seeing Heeney move, he stooped quickly and grasped it in his hand. He was still bent down when Heeney reached him, and he dived forward as the point of the knife came at him. It would have plunged into his side if he had not moved, but the dive saved him. The blade ripped through the fabric of his gaberdine and he felt it gouge his back.

He was on his hands and knees with Heeney on top of him. Heeney struck again with the knife and he put up his left arm to protect himself, so that the sharp steel blade sliced the flesh below the elbow. He scrambled away and turned and threw the lump of concrete. It hit Heeney on the chest and checked him for the moment. Denver heard him gasp and saw him stagger a little but he did not go down.

Denver knew it was only a brief respite and he began to run, seaching for some other weapon which might reduce the odds against him. But it was growing darker all the time, and he tripped on some obstruction and lost his balance. He put out his hands to break the fall and felt the pain in his back and his forearm caused by the impact with the hard floor. He could hear Heeney coming at him again, and he rolled over and saw the man standing over him, breathing hard and with the long knife in his hand.

'I got you now,' Heeney said gloatingly. 'This is curtains for you, Inspector.'

Denver lay where he was, not moving. What could he do now? He was at Heeney's mercy, and looking for mercy in that quarter was like looking for snow in the Sahara.

'Any last words?' Heeney asked. He had the knife poised and was just stretching things out, enjoying his triumph. He was taking his long-awaited revenge now and he meant to relish it; he wanted to see the victim squirm. 'Any messages for posterity?'

He put a knee on Denver's chest and made a sudden lunge with the knife, slashing the other man's left cheek.

Denver saw that Heeney intended keeping him alive for a while in order to make the torment last; a quick death would not have satisfied him; it had to be slow and painful. He could feel the blood running down his cheek, and his arm and back were hurting. He wondered how many cuts Heeney would inflict before delivering the *coup de grâce*, and he gave a sudden jerk with his knees in an effort to dislodge the human burden from his chest. But the effort failed. Heeney just gave a laugh and slashed him on the other cheek.

Denver tried another ploy; he clenched his right fist and struck Heeney in the genitals with all the power he could muster. The punch must have inflicted a deal of pain, and it made Heeney grunt. But he remained kneeling on Denver's chest, and he was so angered by the unexpected blow to this sensitive part of his body that he thought no more about dragging out the torment but only of delivering the final thrust that would set the seal on his vengeance.

Denver saw him raise the knife and he saw it begin its downward movement. He tried to twist out of the way, but could not do so because of the weight on his chest. The point of the knife was coming towards him and he knew that this was the end and that he had accomplished nothing. He was the lamb to the slaughter sure enough, and the lamb had been no help to himself or to Valerie. And Heeney would get away with it again; Heeney the killer; Heeney the clever one. Hell, what a shambles it had turned out to be!

But then he heard a rapid patter of feet; and a kind of shadow appeared behind Heeney and something scythed through the air and hit the killer on the side of the head, so that he fell away from Denver, just fell away out of the line of sight, taking the long knife with him.

Denver rolled over and got up on to his hands and knees, and blood was dripping from his chin and he was feeling as sick as a toad. He stopped there for a moment, trying to get some strength back into his limbs and straighten things out in his mind; and he could hear a lot going on behind him which he could not see: thuds and grunts and heavy breathing and the scuffling of feet. But there was no sound of Heeney's voice and there was no Heeney coming at him any more.

It seemed as though he stayed in that position for a long time, not moving, not doing anything; but it could not have been more than a second or two. Then he got to his feet, swaying a little, feeling groggy and weak in the legs, and in the half-light he could see three young men with cropped heads and Heeney lying at their feet.

It was like some strange tribal rite; the men seemed to be dancing round the body on the ground, and they kept darting in and hitting it with the bludgeons they were carrying, which could have been lengths of wood or bars of iron; and every time a blow was delivered the body seemed to quiver and make a convulsive movement, as though it were about to leap up and join the dance.

But it never did.

And then, with his vision clearing slightly, Denver could see that Heeney's head was nothing but a mass of blood and hair and crushed bone and maybe brains also, so that even his own mother, if she ever got to see him now, would not have recognised her son. And it was no longer a tribal rite but a gruesome nightmare, a horror film to beat all horror films; and he was really sick now, sick to the limit, and he had to turn away so that he could see no more.

He had no idea why it had happened, had no clue as to who these young men were who had come suddenly from nowhere and saved his life. But he remembered the sounds he had heard before entering the building and he guessed that they had been made by the three, who had been waiting outside – not for him but for Heeney. Perhaps they had known Heeney was inside and had been about to go in and deal with him when he, Denver, had turned up and checked them.

So then maybe they had kept watch from the doorway or a window, staying out of sight and coming in to make their attack on Heeney only when his attention had been distracted by other matters so that he was in no position to defend himself. Maybe.

Denver was ignorant of what their grudge against Heeney was; he did not know and did not wish to know. Nor did he know that this piece of wasteland was their hunting-ground and that Heeney had played into their hands by coming there, being so intent on his own affairs that he had forgotten about the skinheads altogether, had in fact written them off as of no account. And so in the event they had been the death of him; the killer had himself been killed.

So maybe he had not been so clever after all.

Denver noticed that the thudding and scuffling had ceased. He turned and saw the three men standing motionless and gazing down at their victim.

One of them said: 'Well, we got him in the end like we said we would. Thought he was tough, di'n't he? Don't look so tough now.'

'That's right,' one of the others said. 'He had it comin' to him.'

The third one said nothing; he just made a giggling sound which was not without a trace of hysteria.

Denver watched them in silence, and all at once they seemed to become aware of his presence. They all turned their heads and looked at him.

'Who are you, mister?' the one who had spoken first asked. He had an oddly sleepy look about him, eyes partly closed, face very pale, albino-like.

'Does it matter?' Denver said.

'It could matter to us.' The man glanced down at Heeney's body and Denver could guess what was passing in his mind. He had been witness to a murder. And it had not been committed to save him; it had just happened that way. People who witnessed murders taking place could find their own lives in danger. It was just one damned thing after another.

'You seen what we done,' the man said. He was holding an iron bar in his hand and half the length of it was smeared with blood. 'That's bad.'

Denver wondered whether the man was high on drugs; whether all three of them were. It was possible.

He felt very tired. It was pointless to think of running away; he was bleeding from four wounds and his legs felt like rubber. He still had the sour taste of vomit in his mouth.

'Not so bad,' he said. 'I won't say anything. You saved my life. I owe you for that.'

The skinhead gave a sneering laugh. He was not buying it and Denver had not expected that he would. There was no way he could make it sound believable.

'We saved your life all right. But maybe that was a mistake. Maybe we should've let him finish you off before we moved in. Maybe it was bad timing. And now maybe we'll just have to complete the job ourselves.'

'If you kill me you could be in real trouble.'

'Wrong, mister. If we don't kill you, that's when we'd be in trouble.'

As with one accord they began to move in on him. The mental picture of himself lying on the ground in the same condition as Heeney flashed into his mind; if this were about to happen might it not have been preferable to die under the knife?

'No!' he said. 'Stop! Don't do it!'

They said nothing. He retreated from them but they came on relentlessly. One of them aimed a blow at him and he had to jump to avoid it. He was unable to dodge the second blow and it caught him on the right arm. The next might find his head and it would be the beginning of the end.

But there was to be no next blow. Miraculously, so it seemed, there were suddenly other men there, some in plain clothes, some in blue uniforms. The skinheads turned, tried to escape, but were caught and overpowered. There came a clinking of handcuffs, gruff words of command.

And then Detective Chief Inspector Rufford drifted
into sight, a little hazily perhaps but none the less welcome for that.

'My God, Roy!' Rufford said. 'You look a mess.'

'In another minute I could have been more of a mess,'
Denver said. 'What kept you?'

He was thankful now that he had had that last change
of mind before leaving the house and had decided to go
by the book after all. If he had not put the call through to
Rufford the police would not have been there now.

'You told us to give you time,' Rufford said. 'You said
you wanted us to keep a low profile because it might be a
delicate operation. Remember?'

It was true, of course; but in the event the profile had
been almost too low. It had been touch and go. If it had
not been for the skinheads they would have been too late.
And then it had been the skinheads themselves who had
been the threat. But it had turned out all right in the end
– more or less.

'How are you feeling?' Rufford asked.

'I've got a cut in the back, a cut in the left arm and a cut
on each cheek. My right arm feels paralysed and I think
my legs have turned to putty. I've been sick and I want to
be sick again. My head aches and I fancy my eyesight is
failing – or it could be the light. Otherwise I'm absolutely
in the pink.'

'Glad to hear it,' Rufford said. 'I was beginning to think
you were not so good. Where's Miss West?'

'I don't know. Heeney knew, but he won't be telling us
now.'

'So we'd better start looking.'

'Yes,' Denver said, 'we bloody well had.'

The police had brought torches and they were needed
now.

Rufford told Denver he had better sit down and take
things easy while they made the search, but he insisted on
going with them. They looked everywhere in the

building and found no Miss West.

'Well,' Rufford said, 'she's not here. What do we do now? Any suggestions, Roy?'

Denver was feeling depressed and deeply worried by the lack of success. The skinheads had been taken away in custody and the murder squad was gathering round the remains of Duggie Heeney, but all that was of no interest to Denver; his one thought was of Valerie West. Some attention had been given to his wounds but blood was seeping through the dressings. Rufford suggested he ought to go to hospital. There was an ambulance waiting, but he refused to get into it.

'He must have hidden her somewhere else. Some other derelict building perhaps.'

'We'll make a search. It may take some time.'

But at that moment a young constable came in and spoke to the chief inspector. 'I think I've found something, sir. If you'll come with me.'

'Lead the way,' Rufford said.

The constable went on ahead and they followed. He led them outside and round the end of the building to a pile of rubble, weeds growing up through it, dripping with moisture. A sheet of rusty corrugated iron was resting against one side of the pile, and the rain was rattling on it and running off in rivulets.

There was a piece of old tarpaulin hanging over one end of the corrugated iron. The young constable pulled the tarpaulin away and shone his torch on a pair of stockinged feet. There were no shoes on the feet and the ankles had been tied together with cord.

'Get that tin off her,' Rufford said.

The constable pulled the corrugated iron sheet away from the pile and Miss West was revealed, gagged and bound, her clothes grimy and dishevelled, her hair tangled and her eyes closed. One side of her face was terribly bruised and swollen and there was a little blood on it.

'I think she's dead,' the young constable said in a stage whisper.

Denver could willingly have strangled him.

NINETEEN

Clean Slate

Maggies Jones read the report in the *Seaport Morning Herald* and called Snappy Deacon's attention to it.

'There's a bit about your friend Duggie Heeney in here,' she said.

'Oh,' Deacon said. He had not even glanced at the paper, otherwise he would have been bound to see it, since it was splashed on the front page. 'What about him?'

'He's been murdered, that's what.'

'Murdered!' Deacon snatched the paper from her and read the report himself. 'Oh, God!' he said.

He did not like it, and his mind was racing as he tried to think of any way this might affect him. He did not see how it could, unless the police got to know he had been friendly with Heeney and came round asking a lot of awkward questions. That might be nasty.

And of course they were bound to connect him with Heeney, because they would look back to the time when the two of them had been sent down for that warehouse job. Hell!

'I'm not sorry,' Maggie said. 'I never did like him. I think he had a bad influence on you.'

'Bad influence be damned! He never had any influence on me at all.'

'If you say so. But I'm glad he won't ever be coming

round here again. He gave me the creeps.'

'So that's something you don't have to worry about no more – creeps. Bully for you.' Deacon spoke sarcastically. 'That makes me really pleased.'

But in fact he was not pleased at all. He was worried. He wondered whether he ought to go and have a word with Mr G; but he could not see how that would help, and he had a feeling that Mr G might not be altogether delighted to see him just now. Why in hell did Duggie have to go and get himself murdered, the stupid idiot.

'Damn him! Damn the silly bastard!'

This outburst caused Maggie to raise her eyebrows, but he offered no explanation. And Heeney still owed him twenty nicker. Well, he could say goodbye to the money now, because Heeney was paying no more debts; he had wiped the slate clean.

But that was the least of Deacon's worries.

Mr G also read the report and was also far from pleased. He summoned Marcus to his presence.

'That gun Heeney used. We've still got it?'

'Yessir.'

'Get rid of it.'

Marcus looked surprised. 'It's a good gun.'

'I don't give a damn if it's the best gun in the world. Get rid of it.'

Marcus gave a shrug. 'If that's what you want.'

'It is. See to it at once.'

Marcus went away to carry out the order.

Mr G sat in his wheel-chair and thought about Heeney. He should never have taken the man on. The fellow had been crazy. He had had a feeling about him at the time but had taken no heed of the instinct that had told him to have nothing to do with him.

And now this.

Mr G was not seriously worried, however; he could see no way in which the death of Heeney could have repercussions for him; the man had been going about his own business when he had met his end and there would have been nothing to connect him with the organisation that was controlled from the big house on Highman's Avenue.

Nevertheless, he did not like it. It was something for which he had not planned and was therefore disturbing. No doubt about it, he had made a mistake in having anything to do with Mr Douglas Heeney.

Denver paid a call on Mrs Heeney. There was no good reason why he should have done so, but somehow he felt an urge to go and see her; it was a way of tying up a loose end.

He had stitches in his back, in his left forearm and in each cheek. He felt like a badly darned sock. But his injuries were not too serious and he had not been detained in hospital.

He drove out to the block of flats where Mrs Heeney lived and went up in the lift with the graffiti and the dirt and the odour of urine. Mrs Heeney was at home but she seemed reluctant to let him past the door.

'What you want with me?'

'Just a little talk. My name's Denver.'

'I know who you are,' she said. 'I seen you before. It was you as went and arrested my Duggie.'

'That was a long time ago. I'm not a policeman now.'

After a while he persuaded her to let him into the dingy living-room. The place was a mess, cluttered with shoddy furniture and other rubbish; dust on everything. Mrs Heeney sat herself down in an old armchair with greasy plush upholstery and stared at Denver, waiting. She was wearing a knitted cardigan, thinning at the elbows, a black skirt and shabby slippers. Her hair looked as if it had not been combed or brushed for weeks; perhaps not washed either.

Denver thought she seemed a trifle afraid of him. She

must have known that her son had inflicted the injuries that were visible on his face, and perhaps she feared he might hold her responsible in an indirect way.

He found a seat for himself and sat down.

'I'm sorry –' he began, and stopped. He could not honestly say he was sorry that Heeney was dead, and she would not have believed him if he had; she could not be so simple as that.

She appeared to guess what he had left unsaid. 'You don't have to be sorry for anything. You was just doing your job when you nicked Duggie, and this time he was the one as started the trouble. He meant to kill you, didn't he?'

'I'm afraid so.'

'Well, it's all over now.'

Denver had the impression that she was relieved to be rid of Heeney. Perhaps he had been a great worry to her when alive. Now she would never have to provide any more alibis for him, never wonder what he might be doing when he was out all night, never worry about the possibility of his being caught and sent back to prison. In many ways her life would be easier without him.

She gave a sigh. 'He wasn't really such a bad boy, you know. He was good to his old mum.'

'I'm glad to hear it,' Denver said.

He wondered who those other four people were that Heeney had killed besides Lacon. Perhaps Mrs Heeney could have enlightened him, and perhaps not. Heeney had probably kept a lot of things from her.

He did not stay long. When it came to the point he could find little to say to her, and he guessed that she wished to be rid of him. She came to the door and saw him out of the flat.

'It'll be quiet here without Duggie,' she said.

Denver thought it was a curious thing to say, seeing that Heeney had spent such a long period away from the place. In a way it would be back to normal.

Though he was not aware of the fact, Mrs Heeney had good cause for saying that her son had been good to her. Turning over the things in his bedroom she had discovered a fat manila envelope stuck to the back of one of the dressing-table drawers with adhesive tape. Inside the envelope were notes to the value of nearly ten thousand pounds.

Mrs Heeney did not know where her son had got the money, but she had no intention of asking any questions about it. The police had not found it when they had searched the room, but they had not been looking for money, only for bloodstained clothing and a murder weapon. Money would have been no clue to Lacon's murderer; it had not been the motive for his killing. He had had nothing.

Mrs Heeney locked and bolted the door after Denver had gone. With all that money in the flat you could not be too careful.

Valerie West was in a private hospital, one of those brand new red-brick buildings which were like luxury hotels. She had been in a coma for two days, and Denver had been worried sick with the thought that she might die without ever regaining consciousness. But she was out of it now and he went to see her after leaving Mrs Heeney.

The room was near the end of a wide corridor, and her name was on the door. He gave a light rap with his knuckles and walked in. It was a good-sized room, with a tall window looking out on to a lawn and flower-beds. There were two chairs and a telephone and a television set, and on one side was a door giving access to the bathroom, *en suite* as the estate agents' advertisements said.

Valerie was awake and propped up on pillows, and he thought she was looking better, although there was still a lot of bruising and swelling on one side of her face, and she had a black eye. He kissed her before sitting down on the chair by the bed.

She said: 'You do look funny with all that stitching on your face.'

'Now see who's talking,' Denver said, and they both laughed.

'What happened to that man?' she asked.

'What man would that be?'

'Heeney. He was the one who did that to your face, wasn't he?'

'Yes.'

'But he didn't kill you. How come?'

'Haven't they told you?'

'Nobody tells me anything. They think it would be bad for me.'

'Then perhaps I hadn't better tell you.'

'If you don't I'll scream the place down. It's driving me crazy, not knowing.'

'Well, I certainly don't want you to go crazy, so I'll tell you. Heeney got himself killed instead.'

She stared at him, wide-eyed. 'You?'

Denver shook his head. 'Not guilty. It was some yobboes who did it. I think he'd done something to annoy them. That was the kind of man he was.'

'And they killed him just for that?'

'Yes. They seemed to feel rather strongly about it. Then they were going to kill me.'

'Why? What had you done to them?'

'Nothing. I just happened to be there when they did for Heeney.'

'Oh, I see.'

'Fortunately for me, the United States Cavalry rode up in the nick of time.'

She looked puzzled. 'Cavalry?'

'Disguised as British Bobbies.'

'You idiot,' she said. And after that she was silent for a while and seemed to be thinking, possibly about what he had told her.

'Now you tell me something,' Denver said. 'Would you have any strong objections to marrying a man with scars on both his cheeks?'

'I'm not sure I could live with him,' she said.

'But you have been living with him.'

'Have I? Well, I suppose that does make a difference. I shall have to consider it.'

After a while Denver said: 'You didn't make that trip to London with the Whizzkid after all.'

'No, I didn't, did I?'

'Of course you know he fancies you?'

'Do you think so?'

'I know so.'

'Do you mind?'

'No,' Denver said, 'I don't mind that. Just as long as you don't fancy him. That I really would mind.'

'Darling,' she said, 'he's my boss. We're just good friends.'